"I wondered if you had a suggestion for something Silver wants for Christmas," Wade said. "Something she's been really longing for?"

"She wants a dollhouse," Connie replied. "An original one that's hers alone."

"Yes, now I remember her mentioning that. Maybe I could build one?" He began structuring it in his mind. It would be a replica of this house. "You're quite something, Connie," he said, admiration flooding him. "You've got all of us learning new ways to deal with each other. I appreciate your help."

"I haven't done anything special." Connie kept her head bent, but her red cheeks told Wade everything he needed to know. "I'm just the nanny."

"Hardly," he said as he walked out of his office to find Silver.

He realized how true it was. Silver's nanny had become necessary to all of them. Connie wasn't just doing her job. She was enriching their lives....

Books by Lois Richer

Love Inspired

*Baby on the Way
*Daddy on the Way
*Wedding on the Way
‡Mother's Day Miracle
‡His Answered Prayer
‡Blessed Baby
Tucker's Bride
Inner Harbor
†Blessings
†Heaven's Kiss
†A Time to Remember
Past Secrets, Present Love
‡‡His Winter Rose
‡‡Apple Blossom Bride

‡‡Spring Flowers, Summer Love
§Healing Tides
§Heart's Haven
§A Cowboy's Honor
§§Rocky Mountain Legacy
§§Twice Upon a Time
§§A Ring and a Promise
Easter Promises
   "Desert Rose"
**The Holiday Nanny

Love Inspired Suspense

A Time to Protect
††Secrets of the Rose
††Silent Enemy
††Identity: Undercover

*Brides of the Seasons
‡If Wishes Were Weddings
†Blessings in Disguise
††Finders Inc.
‡‡Serenity Bay
§Pennies from Heaven
§§Weddings by Woodwards
**Love for All Seasons

LOIS RICHER

likes variety. From her time in human resources management to entrepreneurship, life has held plenty of surprises.

"Having given up on fairy tales, I was happily involved in building a restaurant when a handsome prince walked into my life and upset all my career plans with a wedding ring. Motherhood quickly followed. I guess the seeds of my storytelling took root because of two small boys who kept demanding, 'Then what, Mom?'"

The miracle of God's love for His children, the blessing of true love, the joy of sharing Him with others—that is a story that can be told a thousand ways and yet still be brand-new. Lois Richer intends to go right on telling it.

The Holiday Nanny
Lois Richer

Steeple
Hill®

Published by Steeple Hill Books™

STEEPLE HILL BOOKS

Steeple Hill®

Recycling programs for this product may not exist in your area.

ISBN-13: 978-0-373-81519-7

THE HOLIDAY NANNY

Copyright © 2010 by Lois M. Richer

www.SteepleHill.com

Printed in U.S.A.

I am holding you by your right hand—
I, the Lord your God—and I say to you,
Don't be afraid; I am here to help you.
                              —*Isaiah* 41:13

This book is dedicated to my dad. I love you.

Chapter One

"Do you think Daddy got my letter yet, Connie?"

Connie Ladden couldn't bear to quash the hope shining in Silver Abbot's glossy blue eyes, so she brushed the riot of blond curls away from her four—almost five—year-old charge's face and eased onto the bed, next to the little girl.

"Remember, I showed you on the map how far away Argentina is?"

"Uh-huh." Silver nodded solemnly.

Too solemnly for Connie's liking. Silver wanted her daddy, and after two months as nanny for the delightful child, Connie thought Wade Abbot needed to act more like a father and be here for his precious daughter. Still, her job was to help Silver with her life as it was, not the way they wished it could be.

"Well, it's only been about a week since we

mailed it, sweetie. Argentina is a very long way for a letter to go."

Thanks to the courier's emailed confirmation of delivery, Connie knew the package with Silver's recorded message had safely arrived at its destination. But she didn't want to say that. Connie hadn't yet met Silver's father, and she wasn't sure how Wade Abbot would react to his daughter's latest communication.

"It's been ten days. I counted." Silver frowned. "David, at my preschool, told me email is very fast. Do you know how to do email?"

"Yes." Connie smiled at her serious look.

"You could have sent my letter that way, couldn't you, Connie?"

"I guess I could have. But think how nice it will be for your daddy to get an envelope from home, from his own little girl."

David Foster, Mr. Abbot's lawyer and Silver's guardian, had made it clear when he hired Connie and provided Wade Abbot's email address that Silver's father did not want to be distracted by everyday minutiae. Wade Abbot was in Argentina on a very tight schedule. It was urgent that he bring in the project on time for Abbot Bridges, Inc., according to David. The way he'd phrased it had led Connie to deduce that the company stood to lose a substantial amount of money and perhaps forfeit future contracts with the Argentinean government if the deadline was missed.

"Your daddy might not have had a chance to open it yet."

"'Cause he's so busy." Silver sighed. "I know." Resigned, she snuggled into her bed and drew her puffy pink quilt up to her chin.
Connie bent to kiss her good-night a second time, unable to resist the downy softness of Silver's rounded cheek or the delight of another hug.

"Can't we have just one more story, Connie?" The chubby arms refused to release her neck. "Please?" The beguiling smile begged her to relent.

"You've already had three stories, munchkin. Now it's bedtime. You know my rules." Connie rubbed her nose against Silver's, unclasped her grasp and tucked her arms beneath the pink quilt patterned with fairy princesses. Tiny silver bells attached to princess shoes tinkled softly. "We have a lot to do tomorrow. It's our bird-watching day. I want to find out more about the hummingbirds here in Tucson. You need to rest those baby-blue eyes so you'll be able to point them out."

"You sure like hummingbirds."

"I sure do," Connie agreed.

"Hey, we forgot to say my prayers." Silver grinned.

"So we did. Okay, go ahead." Connie knelt at the side of the bed, closed her eyes and waited.

"Dear God, thank you for today. And for Connie. I love her lots."

Connie's heart squeezed so tight that she could barely breathe. *It's mutual, kiddo.*

"We had fun flying our kites this afternoon, God. Thanks for the wind and for Cora's yummy muffins and for Hornby's pretty roses. Bless my daddy and bring him home soon. And help Granny Amanda not to be mad at Daddy anymore. Amen."

"Amen." Connie hesitated as she studied Silver. "Honey, why do you think your grandmother is mad at your father?"

"Because she said—" Silver's blue eyes welled with tears and she snuffled, unable to finish her sentence. "I don't believe he'd forget about me," she muttered defiantly a moment later. "My daddy loves me. Doesn't he, Connie?"

"Of course he does, sweetie. Everybody knows that. You must have misunderstood your grandmother." Connie hugged the fragile body close, praying her words were true. "Why, look at all the lovely things your daddy sends you. Your room is going to burst if he doesn't stop."

That made Silver smile. A few moments later, her eyelids drooped and she was asleep. Connie rose, switched the lamp to dim and padded quietly out of the room. She set the door just the tiniest bit ajar so that if Silver woke during the night she would see the hall light and not be afraid.

Connie paused, debating the wisdom of her next move. But she couldn't put it off any longer. Something had to be done. Her job was to protect Silver.

Help me, Lord.

She trod downstairs, moving silently over the glossy hardwood until she came to the living room. She tapped on the door once then waited for an invitation to enter.

"Constance. Is everything all right?" Amanda Abbot glanced up from the magazine she was perusing. She'd spilled her tea over the lovely rose-wood table and onto the white carpet but seemed oblivious to the mess.

"Oh, dear." Connie stemmed her irritation and grabbed two napkins to sponge up what she could. "I hope that doesn't mark."

"Who cares? Wade can afford another one." Amanda waved an irritated hand. "What did you want, Constance?"

Connie rose, inhaled and prayed for courage. Some noise outside the room drew her attention for a moment. Probably Cora, the Abbot's cook, leaving for the night.

"Well?" Amanda's eyes flashed with annoyance. "Speak."

"I wanted to talk to you—" Connie gulped and forced herself to continue "—about Silver."

"What about her?" Amanda continued to flip through the magazine. "Is she sick?"

"She was upset by your comments about her father." There, she'd said it.

"My *comments?*" Amanda's lips tightened. She tossed the magazine away. "What comments, exactly, Constance?"

"Actually, it's Connie. Plain old Connie." She cleared her throat. "I believe you hinted that her father had forgotten about her. Silver was quite agitated by that."

"Oh, fiddle." Amanda huffed. "The child needs to hear the truth. As it is, she lives in a fairy tale world. It's better to face reality."

"But it isn't reality, is it?" Connie asked quietly. "Her father couldn't have forgotten about her when he sends her a gift every week."

"Are you questioning me?" Amanda sounded outraged. "You know that you only have this job because I allow it. I could have suggested many others to be my granddaughter's nanny."

But none of them would put up with your manipulations. It was the truth, but Connie didn't say it. Amanda did not like to be contradicted.

She also did not like her stepson.

Or so it seemed to Connie.

"I believe Mr. Foster hired me because he knew

I'd protect Silver. I'm not questioning you. I'm simply telling you that when you say these things about her father, it hurts Silver. And I know you don't want to do that." Connie paused to gather her courage. "Yesterday, you said her father had probably found another family in Argentina. Perhaps you didn't mean for her to overhear, but she did, and she cried about it for an hour."

"Then you weren't doing your job, were you?" Amanda didn't look fazed by her part in her granddaughter's unhappiness. "You're supposed to keep her busy and happy."

"I'm trying to do that. I care a great deal for Silver. That's why I've come to ask you to be more careful." Connie refused to back down. "What you say could damage the relationship between Silver and her father. That's not right."

"What I say is none of your business. Pack your things and get out. You're fired."

Connie wanted to protest, but she knew it wouldn't help. Amanda was not one to be swayed by others.

"I'm sorry if I've offended you," she said quietly. "I'm only trying to do what's best for Silver. That is why I was hired, isn't it?"

"Yes, it is. Isn't it, Amanda?"

Connie whirled around at the quiet but controlled voice that had come from behind her. A man identical to the picture on Silver's night stand dropped the bag he was carrying beside his feet. He held out one hand.

"I'm Wade Abbot. I assume you are Connie Ladden, Silver's nanny."

"I am." She shook his hand, felt the strength in his tanned fingers. He was so rugged looking and so handsome. A tiny shiver wiggled its way from her hand to her heart in a twitch of awareness. "I'm pleased to meet you. Your daughter talks about you constantly. She adores you."

"Does she?" He studied her for a few moments then inclined his head. "I'd like to speak to my stepmother privately, Ms. Ladden. But when I've finished, I'd also like to talk to you. Could you meet me in the kitchen in a few minutes? I've been flying for seventeen hours and I'm starved."

"Certainly, Mr. Abbot."

"It's Wade."

"Yes, sir." Connie forced herself not to look at Amanda as she left the room. She hurried down the hall, pausing momentarily to glance at herself in a mirror. She wished she'd had time to do something about her ponytail and lack of makeup before meeting Silver's father. Not that it mattered. She was just the nanny.

And that's all she intended to be. Romance was highly overrated.

"You're not hungry again, are you?" Cora grumbled when she saw Connie. But her eyes twinkled.

"Because if you are, I've left some chocolate cake in that cupboard."

"Great. I'll cut some for Mr. Abbot. He's talking with Amanda just now, but I'm to meet him here. He's hungry."

"Wade's back? Wonderful." Cora's round face wreathed in smiles, then as quickly saddened. "If I'd known earlier I'd have made his favorite pie, but…" She glanced at the clock.

"You have your granddaughter's recital tonight, right? Don't worry. I'll heat some leftovers for him." Connie hugged the older woman and helped her into her coat. "Go on now."

"You're such a dear. This house has been filled with light and joy since you've come." Cora hugged her back then frowned. "But there aren't any leftovers to heat."

"Then he'll get eggs. I'm not a fantastic cook like you, but I can manage to scramble some eggs. Leave it to me."

"Thank you, dear. I believe I will. Bless you." The woman hurried away.

Connie assembled ingredients, set the kettle to boil and prepared the toaster. But when the slam of the front door shook the house, she decided to check on Silver. If she hadn't already been awakened, the child would be overjoyed tomorrow when she learned her father was home.

Upstairs, Connie noticed Silver's door was open

wider than she'd left it. She hurried toward it then froze. Wade Abbot stood beside Silver's bed, watching as the little girl slept. He stretched out a hand as if to touch her hair then quickly drew it away. Instead, he squatted beside the bed, apparently content to stare.

He was a tall man with dark brown hair cut short, probably to stem the riot of curls that now caressed the tips of his ears. Lean and fit, he had the kind of physique that came from hard physical labor. His shoulders stretched his faded chambray shirt, which he'd tucked it into a pair of well-worn jeans. His feet were covered by battered brown boots. Nothing about him gave away his status as head of a prestigious contracting firm.

Earlier, Connie had only caught a quick look at Wade Abbot's face, but now with Silver's bedside lamp illuminating it, she saw deeply set eyes beneath a broad forehead, chiseled cheekbones above gaunt hollows, a straight aquiline nose with a mustache beneath that partially hid his lips and a jutting chin that telegraphed grit and determination.

In slow motion he lifted something bright blue and fuzzy that released a faint tinkle. Another of Silver's beloved bells? He set the stuffed animal beside his daughter. Then he tenderly lifted her covers and snugged them in place under her chin.

Connie knew very little about the Abbot family.

David Foster had told her that Mrs. Abbot had died four years ago on a yacht in Brazil shortly after Silver's birth. Connie knew from her internet search that the couple had been living in Brazil at the time Mrs. Abbot had died, but she'd found few other details.

Silver remembered nothing of her own mother, which was probably why she yearned for her father so much. But David Foster had warned Connie that the last nanny had left because she'd developed an affection for Wade. He'd been adamant that Connie should not suffer the same fate.

Wade isn't interested in love, so don't have any illusions about him.

As if Connie needed that warning. She wasn't about to give her heart to any man again. Not after being jilted at the altar by a man she'd called a friend for years, a man she'd thought she could trust completely. He was the second important man in her life to let her down when she most needed him. Connie didn't need a third lesson.

"I didn't waken her." Wade now stood beside her in the hallway, his brown eyes swirling with secrets.

"It wouldn't have mattered if you had," Connie murmured, smiling. "She's been longing to see you. She'd be ecstatic."

"But her rest would be disturbed. I don't want that. I'll wait till morning." He took one last look at the sleeping child then motioned for Connie to precede him down the stairs. "She looks well. And still crazy for bells?"

"Oh, yes." Connie chuckled. "She'll be delighted with the toy." She motioned him to a chair at the counter and poured a mug of tea. "I'll scramble some eggs."

"Please, don't bother. I can have toast. Or anything."

"It's no bother. I told Cora I'd do it, because she had to leave to attend a function for her grand-daughter. In fact, I have to do it or she'll punish me tomorrow. I don't want that. Her cooking is to die for." Connie grinned at him then set the pan to heat while she whipped the eggs and added onions, cheese and peppers. "Are you finished with the bridge?"

"You sound like Amanda." He chuckled at her blink of surprise. "Yes, it's finished. A month early, too. Tell me about Silver."

Connie had been prepared to dislike this man. After all, he'd left his little daughter alone for several months to complete a job in some distant country. She didn't see that as the sign of a doting father. But the eagerness in his question now had her reassessing her judgment. She knew nothing about the reasons Wade had left, and she didn't trust the nasty hints Amanda had dropped. Not everyone was like her own father. Why did she have to keep reminding herself of that?

"Silver's very bright. She seems to enjoy her gymnastics club, storytime at the library and her art class."

"So she said. Clever idea, that video you sent. I should have thought of it before. I could have sent one back to her, shown her where I was working, what I was doing." He frowned and then sipped his tea.

"Well, you can do that next time you go. She'll love it." Connie flipped the omelet onto a plate and set it in front of him.

"I'm not going again," Wade said, with a stern finality, as if he thought she'd argue.

"Oh." What were the implications of that? Would Connie's job be over now that he was home? "Silver will be very happy you're staying."

"Mmm." He ate for a few minutes, devouring the omelet and toast she set before him as if he hadn't seen food in a long time. "Sorry." He caught her staring and grinned. "I never eat on airplanes. Your cooking is very good."

"They're eggs. Hard to ruin." She shrugged. "Cora said there's cake. Would you like some?"

He nodded, and she cut a huge slice. Wade lifted a forkful of cake into his mouth, closed his eyes and groaned.

"Man, I've missed this."

"Were there rough conditions where you were working?" she asked, trying to think of a way to ask if she should look for new employment.

"It was a work camp. Most of the labor was Argentinean so the kitchen tried to stick to their culturally familiar food. Delicious, but different." Wade grinned. "I was more than ready for some good old American chow." He finished the cake then set his dishes in the dishwasher.

"I could do that."

"It's done. Perhaps we can talk in the family room." He lifted his cup and walked toward the big sunken room that overlooked the pool and the backyard. He waited for Connie to sit, then sank down in a larger chair. "On the video, Silver mentioned a Christmas play."

"Yes. I've been taking her to church with me on Sundays. The Sunday school is putting on their usual nativity play. They've asked Silver to be one of the Christmas angels. She has a speaking part that she's very excited about." Connie frowned. "I hope it's okay that I took her to church. Mr. Foster didn't object and your—er—Amanda didn't seem to care."

"It's fine," he said. "I should have seen that she was going to Sunday school regularly. My father would have insisted on that."

"Was he a godly man?" she asked curiously.

"My father thought God directed everything in

a person's life if they were committed to Him," Wade told her, his face thoughtful. "I've been remiss in several areas where Silver is concerned, and church is one of them. I regret that."

"Now that you'll be staying home, I suppose I'm out of a job," Connie said, summoning a smile.

"Why would you think that?" Wade regarded her with that dark probing gaze.

"Well, you'll be here and…" Connie stopped, suddenly realizing that Wade had made no mention of taking over her duties with Silver. She should know by now that theirs was not a traditional father–daughter relationship.

"I'm going to be very busy finding enough staff to hire for our new job. And Silver still needs someone to look after her. Unless you haven't enjoyed caring for her?" He raised one eyebrow.

"I love being with Silver," Connie said with genuine satisfaction. "She's a fantastic child, well behaved and so easy to teach. It's been a pleasure to be here these past two months. You've done a great job raising her."

"I can hardly take credit for that. Cora's daughter cared for her when we first returned from Brazil. Then when she started her own family, she couldn't manage it anymore so I hired a nanny for Silver, but—" He glanced up, his brown eyes intense in their scrutiny. "David may have explained the problem to you?"

"He said—" Connie blushed. "He said the nanny became enamored of you."

"Interesting way to put it." His mouth twitched. "She thought she was in love with me. I have no time for love, Ms. Ladden." He paused, watching for her response.

Connie wasn't thrown by his comment. "Me, neither."

"Oh? Why is that?" He leaned back, lifted his feet onto an ottoman. "If you don't mind telling me?"

"I don't mind. It's in the past. I've put it behind me." Which wasn't quite true. Being dumped still smarted. "Six months ago I was engaged to be married," she said quietly. "I learned too late that my fiancé expected me to cut all ties with my family."

"Oh?"

"After I finished school, I helped my foster mother care for my foster brother, a ten-year-old boy named Billy with terminal cancer. I thought Garret understood that I couldn't just walk away from Billy simply because I got married. We'd talked about it. I believed he understood my position. Clearly, I didn't appreciate his issues."

Wade said nothing, but his mouth tipped down in a frown.

"I was at the church, ready to walk down the aisle when someone gave me a note. Garret had left town to go on our honeymoon by himself. He didn't want to start our married life in second place, he said."

"Selfish guy."

"That's what I thought. He wouldn't have had long to wait," she murmured, a flicker of sadness tweaking her heart. "Billy died two months later."

"I'm sorry."

"Me, too." Connie tucked away thoughts of the precious little boy. He could have been her own child, so deeply had she loved him. "Anyway, my foster parents had put up a lot of money for the wedding—alot for them that is. I needed to get a job and pay them back."

"So you came to Tucson. I see. But if you've enjoyed your work here, why even think of leaving?" He rubbed his temple as if trying to ease a muscle there. Tiredness revealed itself in the tiny fan of lines on the outside edges of his eyes.

"I guess I assumed that now you're home you'd be more involved with Silver," Connie said bluntly.

"I will be, as my time allows. But I prefer she have full-time care. That would be you, unless you've other plans?"

"No. Uh, I mean, I'm happy to stay on as her nanny."

Actually it would be a relief. After leaving North

Dakota, Connie had specifically chosen Tucson
because she'd tracked her birth father here. Though
she hadn't yet had any success at finding him, she
spent most of her free time searching. Until she
figured out why he'd abandoned her when she was
eleven, Connie knew she couldn't remove the barrier that had kept her from totally adopting the
faith her foster parents had taught her and trust
God in the deepest recesses of her heart. Garret
had ruined any hope she had of trusting a man
again.

"After seeing that video, I know Silver is thriv-
ing under your care. I'd like to ensure she stays that
way. Her happiness is very important to me." The
quiet words hung in the silence. Then Wade rose,
his gaze pensive. "If you'll excuse me now, I've
had a long flight. I'm going to bed. Amanda's gone
out, but she'll be back. Hornby's still around?"

"Oh, yes. Though I doubt he'll still be up."
Connie checked her watch then shook her head.
"No, I'm sure he's asleep now."

"So he still likes to rise before the rest of human-
ity? Some things never change. I suppose he's still
fiddling with those roses of his?" Wade chuckled
as he followed her from the room.

"Yes. He won first place in the horticultural
show last month." She indicated the snapshot she'd
taken, which Silver had insisted on placing on the
hall table. "Now he's preparing for some kind of

Christmas tour. He must have advised you or Mr. Foster about that?"

Wade laughed. Connie couldn't help admiring how handsome he was when the stern lines around his mouth relaxed and his brown eyes lost their shadows.

"Hornby hasn't advised me of his plans in years," he chuckled. "He started here when my grandfather ran Abbot Bridges. I think he still sees me as a boy who's barely tolerated in his precious gardens. Nothing changes for Hornby but his flowers."

"His son visited him last week."

Wade's eyes opened wide. "Jared is back in town? I didn't think he'd ever leave Australia. I'll have to call him up."

"Well, if you'll excuse me?" Connie tried to step around him, but Wade's hand on her arm stopped her.

"So, there won't be any, um, situations, between us that you might mistake?" Wade asked, his gaze direct.

Connie had to smile.

"I'm not looking for a man," she assured him and then realized that wasn't quite true. "At least, I'm not looking for a husband," she amended. "You don't have to worry about my affections, Mr. Abbot. You're quite safe." Then she stepped awkwardly around him and hurried up the stairs to her room next to Silver's, his "good night" echoing around her head.

As she sat in her window seat overlooking the backyard, Connie mused on the changes that would come. The Abbot home was large. The master wing was on the second floor, on the far side of the house, opposite Silver's rooms and hers. The child might have very little contact with Wade unless Connie arranged otherwise.

"There's a problem between the two of them, God," she murmured, watching as Wade emerged on the pool deck ten minutes later. He walked back and forth across the deck, pausing at one end to inspect a bush, then resuming his private stroll. "Some barrier that I don't understand. Help me to help them. Amen."

She didn't turn on the light, didn't prepare for bed, as was her custom. Instead, Connie sat in the dark, watching Silver's father pace across the yard, his steps barely slowing. When he finally sat on one of the chaise longues, the little clock on her nightstand read two thirty.

Yes, definitely something wrong. It wasn't her business, but Connie wanted to help. She knew what it was like to face each day knowing your father didn't care about you, had cut you out of his life. She couldn't let that happen to sweet Silver.

Wade wasn't uncaring. He'd made it a point to visit his daughter, check on her when he arrived home and even bring her a special toy. He'd asked about her welfare, said it was important to him that she be happy. He had to love her.

"He has to, God. Because I don't want Silver to be like me."

Wade climbed the stairs slowly, knowing he should stay away but needing to reassure himself one more time that Silver was all right, that nothing bad had happened to her in his absence. The reports he'd asked David to send were never enough to soothe his imagined anxieties. And the video Ms. Ladden had sent only made his yearning to be near the child that much stronger.

"Can you come home and see me in the Christmas play, Daddy? Please? I'm going to be an angel," Silver had said in the video.

An angel. A gift from God—for him? That was the question.

He slipped through the partially open door and stood gazing down at the wonder that was Silver. From the moment she'd been born, he'd been overwhelmed by her, by the silver-gold hair that had never lost its fat curls, by her enormous blue eyes that peered up at him with utter trust, by the tiny hands that grasped his in complete confidence that he would not lead her astray.

And yet Wade had failed her. At least he felt he had. Though his heart ached to spill out the words of love that had built inside for the past four years, somehow they wouldn't move past his lips.

Because since the day Bella had died, he'd been enslaved by fear.

Fear that Silver wasn't his. Fear that someone else would claim her and he'd lose the only person in his life who truly mattered. Fear she'd never know how much he wanted to be the kind of dad she deserved. With his return home, those fears erupted anew. What had seemed so simple last week in Argentina—coming home, settling down, being a real father—now took on nuances and complications he hadn't imagined.

Bella's child.

Not his daughter, but Bella's child.

As always, Wade's mind traveled back to that day and the phone call that had turned his world on its axis. There had been a fire on a private yacht. A child had survived unharmed. A woman had died. Her death was a result of smoke inhalation, they said. The reason for the fire wasn't known. When Wade arrived on the scene, he'd seen that beside Bella lay the body of the man she'd run to, the man with whom she'd been going to raise Silver.

The nightmare had shattered when Wade had heard the plaintive cries, pleas for someone to help. He recognized Silver's howl immediately. She lay upstairs in her carrier, secured to a chair on the bow of the charred vessel, kicking and bawling at the top of her lungs, guarded by a firefighter. She was fine—unhurt but hungry. Wade had snatched Silver into his arms and left as quickly as he could. The next day he'd flown home.

But in four years, the startling clarity of one image from that day never left Wade's brain, no matter how hard he'd tried to erase it—Bella's man was a young *blond-haired* Adonis whose blue eyes stared lifelessly at him.

That man could have been Silver's father. Silver, the child Wade would gladly give his life for if it would keep her safe and happy.

The beautiful blessed daughter he'd begun to doubt was his own.

Something wet dripped on Wade's shirt and brought him back to the present. Tears. But what good did they do? How could he give up Silver? It would be like ripping out his own heart.

But what if Wade was wrong to keep her? What if he'd torn her away from cousins, aunts and grandparents who would dote on her, fill her life with love—something he had so much trouble showing?

"I can't lose Silver, God. Don't ask that of me. Please."

God hadn't answered Wade Abbot's prayers in a very long time.

Chapter Two

"I have to thank you, David." Wade looked at the man who'd been his best friend since they'd been kids, the only person besides Jared whom he could trust as Silver's guardian. "Miss Ladden seems to be a perfect match for Silver."

"Because of where she grew up, you mean?" David nodded as he adjusted his chair so the sun couldn't reach his eyes in the outside café. "I guess being the eldest of ten foster kids does prepare you for whatever a whirlwind like Silver can throw at you."

"Ten kids? Wow! I didn't know the authorities would allow parents to foster that many children." Wade bit into his pizza.

"According to my investigator, those who run children's services are so delighted with the results of this foster home that they will send as many kids as the Martens family are willing to take.

Martens—that's the name of Connie's foster parents." David signaled for a refill of his iced tea. "Apparently, kids are clamoring to get in there."

"Why?"

"Maybe because they get to live on a big farm in North Dakota with everything a kid could ask for—a creek to swim in, a hill to slide down in winter, lots of woods to hide in and animals galore."

"You sound like you've seen the place."

"I checked it out." David shrugged. "I had my goddaughter to protect, remember?"

Wade met his gaze. "Thanks, man."

"My pleasure." David grinned. "It's a fantastic farm. Not a lot that's modern but the Martens family make up for that. They seem to adore each and every one of their charges, and their kids beg not to be moved. Of the forty kids the family has had over the years, most have gone on to college."

"Including Miss Ladden?"

"No, she stayed after high school to help the Martens family with a special needs kid. And call her Connie. She doesn't stand on formality." David lifted his pizza then winced. "I can understand your reasons for preferring formality after the last nanny, but I'm fairly sure you're safe with Connie. She's had some bad experiences with men.

I can't imagine she's interested in repeating the experience. Has she told you about her father?"

"No." Wade wanted to know more about the vivacious woman who seemed to adore Silver. "She told me about her fiancé bailing though."

"You should ask her about her dad," David said quietly. "She entered foster care when she was eleven and hasn't seen her father since."

Wade couldn't imagine how Connie must have felt. He'd grown up with a beautiful home and parents who made sure he had everything he needed. Things had changed when Amanda arrived on the scene, especially after Wade's stepbrother, Danny, was born. But Wade had never been abandoned.

Until Bella in Brazil.

"That's the reason Connie came to Tucson," David continued. "She's trying to find her father."

Wade frowned. "Why?"

"You should ask her."

"I will," Wade assured him. "But right now I'm asking you."

"I'm guessing she wants some kind of closure." David grabbed another piece of pizza. "What do I know? I'm just a lawyer."

"A very good one."

"Thanks. What are you going to do about the company? You know Amanda won't let your decision to stay here go by without a fight." David sighed. "Dear Amanda. Sometimes I wish your father hadn't left her those shares in Abbot Bridges."

"You and me both." Wade pushed away his plate, refused the dessert their server offered and asked for coffee. He sipped it then pushed it away as well. "The one thing I really miss about Argentina is the coffee."

"Amanda?" David nudged.

"She can't force me to go back," he insisted. "She'll just have to understand that I need to be here for Silver. I'll find someone else to take my place."

"But you've always been the overseas foreman," David said with a frown. "Are you sure you can let go of that?"

"Already have. I asked Hector Salazar to scout out the next location before I left. His work is ahead of schedule. Time means money, and you know how Amanda loves money." Wade grinned. "When the board sees how much we'll save, they'll approve my plans."

"I hope you're right." David didn't look convinced. He checked his watch and laid down his napkin. "I have a meeting in ten minutes. I have to go." He thrust out his hand and smacked Wade on the shoulder. "I'm glad you're back, man. That little darlin' of yours needs her daddy around."

"Thanks." Wade slapped him back, just a little

harder. It was a game they played. Toughest kid on the block. A relic of their past. "I appreciate what you've done for us, David. By the way, any new lady I should know about?"

"Like I've had time?" David snorted, then grinned. "If I could find someone like Connie, I'd make time, though."

"Did you ask her out?" Wade asked, slightly irritated by the thought.

"She's not interested in me. Besides, I'm a lawyer." David rolled his eyes. "Her ex was one."

"Ow!" Wade winced but laughed.

"We legal eagles are always maligned. By the way, I hear Jared Hornby's back. We should get together. It's been too many years since the old threesome hit this town. Let me know if you hear from him." David grabbed his briefcase, waggled his fingers and took off in the long-legged stride he'd once used to great advantage on a varsity football field.

Relishing the relative peace of the sidewalk café after Argentina's hustle and bustle, Wade remained in his chair, sipping coffee that was too weak and thinking.

"Daddy!" The squeal could only belong to Silver. She appeared, dragging Connie by the hand toward him.

Connie carried a large bag. It bumped against bare slim legs, which her lovely yet conservative yellow sundress revealed. The lemony shade enhanced the sunny highlights in her tumble of chestnut curls.

After a moment, Silver found Connie's progress too slow. She let go of Connie's hand and raced up to him, the tiny bells attached to her blue barrettes jingling merrily as she flung her arms around his neck and pressed her lips against his cheek. "Are you meeting us for lunch, Daddy? Is that the surprise, Connie?"

Wade's warning siren went off. Had the nanny arranged this "chance" meeting?

"No! Silver, I had no idea your father—" Connie's flushed face gave away her embarrassment. She glanced quickly at Wade and as quickly away. It was obvious she was recalling his comment from their conversation three nights earlier and was uncomfortable with the current meeting.

Wade returned Silver's embrace then released her as he reconsidered his rush to judge the nanny. He'd told no one he was meeting David. His assistant only knew he was to be out of the office for an hour. Connie couldn't have known of his plans. But a prickle of warning still feathered its way down his nerves. He'd been tricked before. It wouldn't happen again.

"Haven't you eaten lunch yet?" Wade took the parcel from Connie and set it on David's vacated chair. Silver chose the chair across from him, leaving Connie the seat next to his. Wade held it while she sat down, her head tilted to avoid his gaze. But that only gave him a better view of her long, lovely neck.

"I really didn't know you would be here. I had to go to the fabric store on this block. Silver needs an angel costume," she muttered.

"They have those at the fabric store?" Wade motioned for the waiter.

"No. They have fabric," she said, risking a quick look at his face. "I got some yardage. I'm going to make her costume."

"You know how to sew?" Somehow it didn't surprise Wade as much as it should have. From the little he'd seen, Connie Ladden seemed to do many things well.

"Connie makes her clothes, Daddy. Isn't that amazing?" Silver sipped her water, her blue eyes shining.

"Very amazing," he agreed, studying the lines of her dress. Connie blushed even more deeply so he looked at Silver. "What would you like to have for lunch, my treat."

"Can I have a hamburger?"

About to agree to Silver's request, Wade happened to glance at Connie and saw the quick negative shake of her head. He sat back and waited for her to choose Silver's meal.

Connie didn't dictate or order for Silver. She

consulted with her, offering choices. The end result was a healthy blend of several food groups, which the little girl seemed delighted about. For herself, Connie ordered a salad and soup.

"They do a wonderful shrimp salad," Wade told her.

"Thanks, but no thanks." For the first time since she'd arrived, Connie looked directly at him, a smile tipping up her full rosy lips. "I'm afraid I'm allergic to seafood."

"Sad for you," he said with a grin. "Shrimp, lobster, clams—I love them."

"I guess many people do," she mused quietly then quickly glanced away, breaking their gaze.

There wasn't a trace of "feel sorry for me" in her voice, and yet Wade found himself wondering what else this woman had missed out on.

"Daddy?" Silver tugged on his sleeve, drawing his attention. A tiny pleat marred the perfection of her pretty forehead.

"Yes?" Wade wondered if the strong sunshine would mar her skin, but no sooner had the thought crossed his mind than Connie pulled a hat out of her bag and set in on the child's head.

"Me and Connie went to a dancing thing. What did you call it again?" Silver twisted her head to study Connie, her face perplexed.

"Ballet. And we say Connie and I went, not Connie and me." The tiny rebuke was accompanied by a soft squeeze to the shoulder. "It was the Nut-cracker Ballet," Connie explained as their server arrived with their meals. "Silver was quite intrigued by the dancers."

"Yes, and we went behind the stage and saw how everything worked. I loved the Sugar Plum Fairy, Daddy. Could I be a Sugar Plum Fairy, do you think?" She crunched on a carrot then swallowed quickly. "When I get big, I mean. If I practice."

"Ballet is awfully hard work, Silver." Wade glanced at the nanny, hoping for some direction, but Connie was busy squeezing lemon on her salad.

"I'm strong. 'Sides, Connie says that if you don't ever try to do hard things, you won't ever know if you can do them." Silver tipped her head up, a question in her eyes. "Isn't that right, Connie?"

"Yes, honey. But I wasn't referring to ballet," she assured Wade, tilting her curly dark head back so she could look at him full on. "A commitment like that has to be made by you and your father."

Her father. But was he?

"I'll think about it, Silver. Okay?" He waited until she nodded, her cheeks full as a squirrel's storing nuts. He glanced at the clock. "I guess I'd better get back. We have a board meeting this afternoon."

"Oh, can't you stay a few more minutes?" Connie's rushed whisper came as Silver turned away to watch a bird. "You've been away so long, and Silver really needs to reconnect."

She had gray eyes, Wade suddenly realized. True gray, not the changeable shade of blue-gray usually seen. They held his stare unwaveringly, searching his for—something.

Immediately, his hackles rose. He'd been wrong. She had found out he was coming here, had arranged for them to arrive just as David left so she could eat with him and beg him to stay. She hadn't paid any attention to his warning. Wade had a horrible sense of déjà vu.

And he couldn't, wouldn't, allow it.

"I told you, Ms. Ladden. I'm very busy." Wade rose, tossed some bills on the table and pulled on his jacket. "I don't have time to dawdle over lunch with you."

Emphasis on the last two words was lost on her. She leaned back in her chair and studied him for several long moments. Finally she nodded. She looked—sad.

"I see."

Wade heard a wealth of reprimand in the comment and felt a boatload of guilt. He'd only just arrived home. He wanted and needed to spend time with Silver, as she needed time with him. He wanted to see all the nuances of his quickly growing girl. But not now and not with Connie watching.

"I'll see you both at dinner. Be good, kiddo." With an awkward pat on Silver's head, he escaped the nanny's intense inspection.

"'Bye, Daddy." Silver grabbed his hand and pulled on his sleeve, asking him to bend. When he did, she planted her lips against his cheek and gave a loud smack. "You be good, too," she said and then dissolved in a fit of giggles.

"Right." Wade left, striding back to the office as if hounds pursued him. He'd have to warn Connie again. Tonight. Before things got out of hand.

But as he sat behind his desk, thinking about how he should say it, Wade could almost hear David's snickers.

What makes you think she's after you, Abbot? Bit of an egomaniac?

Wade felt a flush of embarrassment. Maybe that was true. But as he walked into the boardroom, he resolved that he was not going to allow a second fiasco. Maybe Connie would think him a self-important jerk, and that was okay.

As long as she didn't start thinking of him in a more personal way, as more than her employer.

"Mr. Abbot says he won't be home for dinner tonight, Connie. He'll get back to you about a time when the two of you can talk."

"Fine." Connie squeezed the telephone tightly while fighting to keep her tone even so Wade's assistant wouldn't guess she was upset. "Would you remind him that if Silver is to start ballet, tomorrow is the last day to register? Thank you."

Two weeks. That's how long Wade Abbot had been avoiding her. But in those two weeks, Connie thought he'd had ample time to make a decision on Silver's request to take ballet lessons. And yet he still hadn't told her his preference.

"When's dinner?" Silver stood in the doorway, trying to stand on her very tiptoes as she'd seen at the ballet and wobbling so badly she gave up. Her tiny sneaker bells "pinged" joyously as she hopped around the room.

"Soon. I told Cora we'd love to have some yummy crow's feet." Connie was beginning to regret attaching those bells to so many things, though they were a good warning system announcing Silver's presence.

"Crow's feet?" Silver flopped down on the floor, crossed her legs and propped her chin on her hands. "That's not a real food. Is it?"

"Of course." Connie hid her smile as she folded the last bits of Silver's laundry. "Crow feet stew, crow feet soup, crow feet casserole. Yum." The teasing games were part of her effort to keep Silver from becoming too intense. Which was happening more and more as her father took pains to avoid Connie, and therefore Silver.

The question was why was he avoiding her?

"You're joking, Connie. I can tell."

"How can you tell?" Connie sank down on the floor across from the little girl and waited.

"When you're joking you get a wiggly kind of a thing at the corner of your mouth. Like you want to giggle but can't." Silver grinned. "You've got it now."

"I guess I'll have to watch myself then." Connie assumed a very stern look then leaned forward and began to tickle the child. "Crow feet juice for you for supper."

"With red-painted toenails," Silver laughed, doubling over and hooting with laughter.

"Is it necessary to make so much noise?" Amanda stood in the doorway, her frown fierce. "I have a terrible headache."

"I'm so sorry. Can I get you anything for it?" Connie offered, springing to her feet.

"How about some peace and quiet?" the older woman snapped as she yanked the bedroom door closed. The slam reverberated to the bells on Silver's shoes.

"Now *my* head hurts." Silver sighed. "How much longer is it until Daddy comes home, Connie?"

"I don't know, sweetie. Your daddy is very busy."

"I'm tired of busy." Silver pressed her nose against the window, her voice drooping as much as her body. "I thought that when Daddy was home I would see him a lot, but he's never home."

"I know it seems like that," Connie murmured, drawing the child into her arms. "But I'm sure it's only while he gets things organized. You have to be patient and keep praying that God will help." She hated saying those words. Why should a child have to beg for her father's attention?

"I have been praying. But I think God is busy, too." Silver sighed heavily.

"God is never too busy to hear our prayers, sweetheart. Never ever. Okay?" She chucked the girl under the chin. "I'm hungry. Let's go see if our crows are cooked."

"Okay." Silver accepted her outstretched hand and swung it as they walked downstairs. "Tonight's the night Cora tucks me in, isn't it?"

"Because it's my night off, yes." Surely she wouldn't have to give up her plans? After many hours of chasing disappointing leads, Connie had finally tracked her father to a soup kitchen. She hoped this evening might render a clue to his current whereabouts.

Please don't let Silver make a fuss tonight.

The prayer had no sooner left her lips than guilt descended. The last thing Connie wanted was for Silver to feel like her nanny was too busy for her, too.

"I was going out after dinner, but if you want me to stay—"

"No. I'm a big girl. And I love Cora." Silver paused on the landing. Her voice dropped to a whisper. "But she doesn't read stories as good as you."

"Tomorrow we'll do a little extra reading, okay?" Connie promised.

"Okay." Silver smiled, but it was obvious by her quick scan of the hallway and front rooms that she was still thinking about her father's frequent absences.

Silver's appetite lacked its usual exuberance, and when Cora finally appeared for storytime, the child docilely handed her the book and leaned back against her pillows after kissing Connie goodnight.

She was so polite, Connie mused as she made her way across Tucson to the soup kitchen, hoping to talk some more with the man who claimed to have spoken to her father. Too polite. Totally unlike the usually bouncy, boisterous little girl who reached out and grabbed at life.

Connie stepped into the old church and scanned the fellowship room. She would have to talk to Wade tonight. For Silver's sake. She'd have to tell him that his daughter needed him to pay her some attention. How hard could that be?

No harder than questioning total strangers about

a father who'd abandoned her eleven years ago, a man she barely remembered. A man from whom she desperately needed answers.

Compared to that, facing Wade would be a cakewalk.

Chapter Three

It was late and he was dead tired, but Wade plowed through the water anyway, forcing his arms to reach and pull, praying swimming would ease the tension of his body long enough for him to sleep.

Amanda had been at her finest today, pushing all his buttons with her references to the past, to the accident that had killed her husband and her son, both deaths she blamed on him.

"You killed my family."

"My family, too," he'd reminded her. *"Someone ran into us, Amanda. I didn't do anything wrong."*

But the words had rung hollow the first time Wade said them six years ago, and time hadn't made them sound any better. He should have avoided the accident—somehow.

Winded and too tired to continue, Wade dragged himself out of the water. It took only minutes for the dry Arizona air to suck away the moisture. Then he pulled on his shirt and jeans over his swimsuit and stretched out on a lounger, staring at the stars above.

Where was God in all of this recrimination, he wondered. Did God blame him for killing his own father? Is that why Wade seldom felt comfortable in the home he'd loved as he grew up? Was that why he kept himself constantly on the go, to escape the guilt?

"Have I done something wrong?"

Wade's eyes popped open. He jerked his head to the side, not needing to see her to know that Connie Ladden stood nearby. She wore jeans and a T-shirt, but not the slick form-fitting jeans most women favored. Instead Connie's jeans looked elegantly tailored. He wondered if she'd sewn them herself, and then he told himself to focus.

"Is it so bad that you can't even speak to me?"

"Excuse me?" Wade blinked, trying to reorient his thoughts. "Is what so bad?"

"Whatever it is that prohibits you from extending the common decency of answering my phone calls." She was angry, evidenced by the rigid way she lowered herself onto the chaise next to his, and the glittering silver sheen of her gray eyes. Also, her mouth was pursed in a thin tight line.

"What calls?" He frowned, rubbed his forehead. "What was it you wanted?"

"Unbelievable." She glared at him. "Absolutely unbelievable."

It was not the time to speak, so Wade shut up and waited for enlightenment.

"I've been trying to get your consent for Silver's enrollment in ballet. We talked about it that day at lunch two weeks ago, remember?"

A flicker of a memory returned.

"I'm sorry. I didn't realize you were waiting for my approval," he said finally. "I assumed you would proceed as usual and decide the matter for yourself."

"But—" Connie frowned, peering at him through the dim light "—you're her father, and you're home now. The decisions about her should be yours."

"And I am authorizing you to make them." He swung his legs off the chaise, preparing to leave.

"Don't you care about Silver at all?" The almost-whisper hit him like a baseball bat.

"Of course I care about her!" He rose, glared down at her. "How dare you—"

"I dare because I love that child. Her heart is breaking, because she never sees you. It's as if you're still in Argentina, only she doesn't get the gifts anymore." Connie rose too, eyes blazing. "She loves you so much, but you seem to have abandoned her."

"Like your father abandoned you?" He regretted

that the moment the words left his lips, but it was too late to take them back. "Connie—"

"Exactly like that." She straightened and thrust her chin forward as if to repel his next attack. "At least I was eleven. Silver isn't even five."

"I shouldn't have said that."

"Why not? It's true." Connie's gaze dropped. "I was abandoned, left on a street corner outside a church in Grand Forks on Christmas morning." That wound had never quite healed. "I couldn't bear it if Silver had to go through what I did."

"She won't."

"She will if you don't show her how much you care," Connie insisted.

Wade already had enough guilt about the way work had taken over the moments he'd planned to spend with Silver. He couldn't let Connie think— what, that he didn't love the child? But that was exactly what he was afraid of saying. He was scared that the heart-wrenching adoration he felt for that tiny child would kill him when he finally found Silver's real family and she left.

"What is wrong?"

He blinked and opened his mouth to tell her to butt out.

"Don't try to blow me off. I've seen you sneak into her room at night and watch her. That's not the action of a man who doesn't care." Connie sat down again. "Yet you refuse to make time for her. Why?"

He studied her, and like a thief, the notion crept into his brain—maybe this was Connie's way of getting close to him. Maybe she was so anxious to find common ground between them that she was conning him into trusting her.

"Something's changed? What is it?" Her big gray eyes blinked up at him.

"Ms. Ladden. I thought I had made it clear that there can be no relationship between us. I'm just not interested."

Her eyes widened. She froze for a moment then laughed. Her face was flushed a brilliant red, but embarrassment didn't stop Connie from speaking her mind.

"You idiot!" She stepped closer until they were almost nose to nose. "I'll tell you one last time that I am not chasing you. I am not interested in you, Wade Abbot. I could never even consider a relationship with a man who leaves his daughter behind for months on end while he chases off to some foreign country."

"Now wait a minute. You don't understand—"

"Just to make this very clear," she interrupted his explanation, her tone scathing, "I certainly wouldn't bother myself over a man who ignores a sweet little girl so badly that she goes to bed every night asking herself what she has to do to gain her father's love." Connie stepped back. Her voice dropped. "Believe me, Mr. Abbot, you're just not that appealing."

Then she turned and walked away.

"I'm not sure Silver is my daughter."

The words pinged into the silence of the night like resounding gongs. Connie jerked to a halt and stood there, with her back to him, for perhaps ten seconds. Then she turned.

"Why don't we go inside?" she said quietly, her expression blank. "I'll make us something to drink. Then perhaps we can hash this out." Her eyes met his and held. "Because there is no way in this world that Silver is not your daughter. No way."

A second later, she'd disappeared into the hedge, no doubt headed for the kitchen.

Wade had finally said it out loud, at last admitting the one thing he most feared.

"I've just given her a reason for us to work together," he muttered as he climbed the back stairs to his room. "How stupid can I get?"

Stupid, maybe. But it was also a relief. He'd assumed, though it hurt him deeply, that the best thing was to stay away from Silver, not let her get too attached in case he eventually managed to do the right thing and return her to her real family.

He had a hunch Connie was going to tell him that was the wrong approach.

* * *

I'm not sure Silver is my daughter.

The starkness of Wade's voice when he'd said that still hurt Connie's heart.

A thousand questions tumbled around in her brain, but she stuffed them back and concentrated on mixing the hot chocolate packets with hot water.

Help me help him, Lord. Let me be a ray of light in his darkness.

"Miss Ladden—"

"Whenever you want to reprimand me, or when you suspect me of something, you always call me Miss Ladden. My name is Connie. And let's get one thing clear." She motioned for him to sit on one of the stools. "I am not here for any reason but that I want Silver to be happy. In order for that to happen, she needs her daddy. Okay?"

He nodded, took the cup she offered and began idly stirring it.

"So?" She sipped her hot chocolate and waited.

"I don't know where to start."

"Start with why you left Silver here when you went to Argentina," she suggested.

"She was two. There was unrest in the country. I was working in a desolate region. It was no place for a child. To leave her in the city—" He shrugged. "Kidnappings are not uncommon in Argentina."

"But then why go there in the first place?" Connie hoped he'd explain and not tell her it was none of her business—which it wasn't.

"I didn't have a choice." Wade sighed, took a sip of his drink and began his story. "My father was not young when he met and married Amanda. I was twenty-four when their son Danny was born."

"Was Danny a problem for you?" she murmured.

"No." He smiled. "Danny was a sweetheart. Nobody who met him didn't love that kid. He was a firecracker, and I adored being his big brother." The smiled faded. "Danny and my father died in a car accident. And Amanda blamed me."

"Why?"

"I was driving the car that night."

The stark pain in those words kept Connie silent. She prayed wordlessly.

"It was my dad's birthday. He loved golfing, so we'd spent the day at the golf course. Of course Danny had to come, too." Wade's lips twitched upward for a second. "The kid was a natural."

Silence yawned. But Connie didn't break it, sensing that Wade needed to do this in his own time, his own way.

"It started to rain—hard. I would have pulled over, but Dad wanted to get back home. Amanda had arranged a birthday party and he didn't want to be late for it." He took a deep breath and said the rest in a rush. "A car came up too fast behind us, slid into us and pushed us into oncoming traffic. Dad had turned, trying to calm Danny. The impact forced a rib into his lungs, which collapsed."

"And Danny?" Connie held her breath.

Wade looked straight at her, his face like stone, his body hunched over as if he'd been struck.

"His seat belt came undone. Amanda later claimed it had never been done up. Danny was thrown from the car. He died." His white face barren of all expression, Wade continued. "Amanda couldn't forgive me. With Dad's shares, she had a majority in the company. To punish me, she persuaded the board that I was needed in Brazil to finish a project. I didn't argue. I just wanted to get away."

He needed something to draw him from his private agony.

"Brazil is where you met your wife," Connie said.

"Bella. Yes." He nodded. But the joy she'd expected to see in his eyes wasn't there.

"What was she like?"

"Beautiful in an exotic kind of way. Long, curly black hair and olive skin. Dark expressive eyes. Very Latin in demeanor. Bella loved to dance. She was always the highlight of any party." The words came out like little staccato beats, without expression.

"And you had Silver."

"Yes." Wade smiled, but he didn't continue. Why? Was his wife's death too painful?

"Bella liked being a mom?"

"At first you could hardly get Silver out of her arms."

At first, Connie noted. "You were happy?"

"I thought so." Wade looked straight at her. "I had to be at the work site in the country during the week, but I always returned to Rio on the weekends." He swallowed. "One Friday I came home and there was a note. Bella had left me and taken Silver. I'd barely read it when the police called. She and the man she was leaving me for were dead. Smoke inhalation from a fire aboard their yacht. Mercifully, Silver was fine. I took her and came back home."

"But you didn't stay in Tucson."

Wade shook his head.

"Can I ask why?"

"Why?" A wry half smile tilted his mouth. "I was very successful in Brazil. Profits were pouring in. I'd landed a whole new contract, bigger and better in Argentina. No way did the board want me at home."

The board or Amanda? Connie mulled over his words, her brain assembling the pieces.

"I was ordered back."

"So you left Silver here because you were

worried about her safety," she surmised, waiting for his nod. "What about Bella's relatives?"

"Bella came from a very poor family. She had two sisters, but they were struggling with their own lives. They didn't want a niece to add to their baggage."

"It's sad they've missed out on so much," she murmured. "Knowing Silver is something to be cherished."

He looked at her, relief dawning. "Yes."

Connie waited and waited, but Wade said no more. He finished his drink and pushed the mug away. She was going to have to press for more details.

"But why would any of that make you think you aren't Silver's father?"

Wade said nothing at first. After a moment, he walked around the breakfast bar and pulled a snapshot of Silver off the fridge. He held it up next to his face.

"Notice any similarity?"

Connie glanced from him to the picture and back. Finally, she shook her head. Wade reached into his pocket and pulled out his wallet. He removed a small square and set it on the granite countertop.

Connie sucked in her breath, stunned by the beauty of the woman smiling at the camera.

"Bella. She was very beautiful."

Wade didn't speak. He simply set Bella's picture next to Silver's. The truth hit Connie like a sledgehammer.

"Bella's boyfriend?" she whispered. "The one who died?"

"Bingo. Blond hair, blue eyes." Wade's face didn't alter as he returned the photos to their respective places. Then he sat again. "Now you understand."

"I don't really," Connie murmured, unable to absorb the implications of his words. "There are such things as recessive genes."

"As far as I know, there has never been a blond in my family. I'm sure the same is true for Bella's."

"But your name is on the birth certificate, isn't it?"

He nodded.

"Then you're Silver's parent. Who could dispute that?"

"A word on a piece of paper doesn't make a lie true."

Connie opened her mouth, but the words she'd been about to utter got stuck when she saw Wade's face. Stark pain bled from his expressive eyes.

"I can pretend I'm her father, but that doesn't make it so."

"Pretend?" She leaned forward to peer into his face. "Are you only pretending?"

"No! But—" he shrugged his shoulders, sighed. "Don't you see my problem?"

"No, not really," she admitted. "You have been the custodial parent of record for her entire life. Silver is healthy, happy and settled in the home that you've provided for her. Contesting that would be difficult."

Wade blinked. "How do you come to know so much about parental rights, Connie?"

"Hang around long enough in the foster care system and you become very familiar with all the legal mumbo jumbo." She tossed him a smile but refocused on Silver's picture. "Have you spoken with David about your worries?"

"I haven't spoken with anyone—until now."

"You have to talk to David. He's a lawyer. He can make sure that no one can question your rights." Something about Wade's face made Connie stop.

"Maybe Silver would be better off with her real family," he murmured.

"You are her 'real' family. She's never known anyone else. Would you actually sit back and let Silver go?" She couldn't believe it. She'd seen Wade's face after he snuck into the little girl's room each night. He loved Silver. "I can't believe you care about her so little."

He hunkered forward, his glare intense.

"It's because I care about her so much that I came back. I bought up shares of the company while I was away. Amanda won't be able to force my hand anymore." His fingers fisted. "But what if Bella's 'friend' had family who would love and protect Silver far better than I'm able to? What if she has half brothers and sisters who would fill her life with love and joy? What if—"

"I can't listen to this." Connie jumped up from her stool. She flung the mugs into the dishwasher and snapped the door closed while struggling to contain her temper. It didn't work. "How dare you?" she sputtered.

"Uh—" Wade's jaw dropped at her ferocity.

"How dare you refuse the wonderful gift God has given you? How dare you even imagine that God would allow you such a precious child without giving you whatever is needed to raise her?" Connie glared at him. "Your biggest problem isn't your father's or Danny's or Bella's deaths, Wade. Your biggest problem is you are afraid to give a wonderful little girl who asks nothing of you the one thing she craves. You're a chicken. You can hardly wait to dump Silver on somebody else so you can hightail it back to South America and continue your isolation."

"Now just a minute—"

"Isn't it true?"

"No!" He was standing now, too, his face furious. "I'm trying to do what's right for her."

"Like you were trying to do what was right

for the last nanny when you had David fire her?"
Connie shook her head. "You'll do almost anything
to avoid commitment, won't you? You're like some
of the parents who let their kids grow up at my
foster parents' home because they were too selfish to expand their lives to include everything that
goes along with having a child in their world."

"Parents like your father, you mean?" Wade
snapped.

Connie ignored the bite of pain and nodded.

"Exactly like him. Tonight I spoke to a man
who knew my father. Do you know what he told
me?"

"I have a feeling you'll explain."

She ignored the snarly tone of his voice, because
she knew he was hurting.

"Eleven years ago my father found out he had
cancer. He dumped me because he was afraid he
wouldn't be able to take care of me. He had some
weird notion that it would be better for me to be
taken in by strangers than to spend our last days
together."

"Maybe that was the right decision," Wade murmured frowning.

"It wasn't!" Connie had to make him understand. "If I'd known my father might be dying, I
could have been there, had time to say the things
in my heart and told him I loved him. Instead, I've
spent every night of the past eleven years praying

he survived and dreaming of a second chance to spend just one hour with a man who dumped me because it was easier. I've wasted years wondering where he was, why he didn't come for me, if I wasn't lovable, if I'm always going to be left behind when it comes to the kind of true love that the Bible talks about. The kind that hopes all things, believes all things, endures all things. Self-doubts and a boatload of questions—that's the legacy my father's 'right' decision left me, Wade."

The tears came then, waves of pure sorrow drawn from the well of her pain. And there wasn't a thing Connie could do to stop her heaving sobs.

A terrible silence yawned. Then a moment later, Wade's arms enfolded her.

"I'm sorry, Connie. I'm truly sorry."

After a few blissful moments, she pulled away, furious that she'd done the one thing she'd vowed would never happen with Wade Abbot. She'd allowed herself to act like the previous nanny whom he'd sent away. Now he would be really worried that she was after him.

"I didn't mean—"

"Nobody ever means to hurt people, Wade. But that doesn't stop it from happening." She stepped back, fighting to regain her composure. "Thank you for telling me your problem. I promise I won't share it. But it seems to me that you have a decision to make."

"I do?"

"Yes." She paused, forming the words in her head before she spoke them so their impact would force him to think about the effect of his actions on Silver.

"What decision would that be?" Wade looked impatient and frustrated.

"Whether or not you believe Silver is worth fighting for."

Wade said nothing, simply glared at her. Connie walked upstairs, pausing by Silver's door. She dried her cheeks and smoothed her hair just in case Silver had wakened. Then she stepped inside the room.

The little girl lay curled in her bed, eyes closed, one hand under her rosy cheek, her lips tilted in a smile. She cuddled the parrot Wade had given her under one arm, her soft breathing ruffling its fur.

Connie knelt by the bed and silently poured her heart out to the One who always listened.

"He can't let her go, God. It would hurt Silver so terribly. She loves Wade. She needs him in her life to guide her and love her. Please open his eyes."

She heard the soft muffle of footsteps at the door, but she didn't look up. A few moments later, the steps went away. Connie knew it was Wade, knew he'd been checking on the child he loved, whether he could admit that love to himself or not.

It was clear from his story that Wade had been hurt, badly wounded by the loss of loved ones and the treachery of a woman he'd thought he could trust. In his absence from Silver, those wounds had festered, fed by the poison of self-doubts.

What could she do to help?

When no answers arrived, Connie rose and left the little girl to her rest. She returned to her own room and the window seat where she could gaze at the stars and commune with God.

A lone figure sat on the pool deck, staring into the water, oblivious to the cool wind that had Connie quickly closing her window. Her heart went out to Wade. She had to help. But how?

And then it came to her. Perhaps Wade would think she was following in her predecessor's steps, but Connie was going to spend the next few weeks figuring out ways to get father and daughter together.

"If he can finally understand that no matter whose genes she carries, Silver will never consider anyone but Wade as her father, perhaps he'll understand why he has to be the man she needs."

It was an awesome challenge, especially given Connie's overwhelming reaction to being cradled in his arms. But it was natural, wasn't it, to respond when someone empathized with you?

"Yeah." Her conscience mocked her. "Let's go with that. Let's pretend you didn't enjoy Wade's embrace."

Chapter Four

"What are we doing, Connie?" Silver's bright blue eyes scanned the mess atop the dining room table.

"Preparing for your Christmas party."

"A party?" Silver's blue eyes grew huge. "But it's not Christmas for a long time."

"One month from today is Christmas day." Connie showed her on the calendar. "And the day after Thanksgiving is exactly the right time to start thinking about Christmas." She tweaked the child's nose. "So we have to get busy."

"I can help you?" Silver clapped her hands. A second later she'd pulled up a chair next to Connie's. "Who will come to my party?"

"Well, I think we should invite Hornby and Cora," Connie suggested.

"Yes. And Uncle David."

"Okay." Surely a party would help her charge

forget about her father's inattentiveness for a little while? Relieved the child was getting into the spirit of things, Connie gave her the notepad and helped her write David's name.

"We have to invite David's sister, too," Silver insisted. "Her name is Darla. She had a skiing accident and hurt her head, but she's getting better."

"Is she well enough to come to a party, do you think?" Connie watched anticipation build in the little girl's heart-shaped face.

"Yes!" Silver jiggled in her seat, her excitement setting the tiny bell on her jeans' pocket tinkling. They added Darla's name to the list.

"Who else would you like to invite?"

"Grandma?" Silver whispered with a glance over one shoulder. "It wouldn't be nice to have a party and not ask her."

"No, it wouldn't," Connie agreed, wondering if Wade's cranky stepmother would put in the effort to show up, especially since her histrionics yesterday had spoiled Cora's lovely Thanksgiving meal.

"Grandma's always sad," Silver said. "Maybe a party will make her happy."

"Maybe it will." Privately, Connie doubted that.

"Can I invite the kids from my preschool?"

"Oh, sweetie, I'm not sure—"

"What's going on here?" a low voice demanded.

"Daddy!"

Connie flinched in surprise. She'd come up with the party idea hoping to surprise Wade with a fait accompli, so that he wouldn't have time to think up a refusal to help. The man never showed up at home midafternoon. Why today?

"We're planning my Christmas party, Daddy." Silver bounced off her chair and raced over to him. "It's going to be so fun."

"A party, huh? When is it?" He chucked Silver under the chin awkwardly and smiled at her giggles.

Connie gave him credit for at least trying to be fatherly.

"I don't know." Silver grabbed his hand and pulled him toward the table. "But you can help, Daddy."

"Me? But I can't." He looked terrified. "I have to—"

"Please, Daddy?" Silver wheedled. "We have so many things to decide," she said in a parrot-like voice that Connie recognized as mimicking her own.

"I'm sure." Wade looked like he wanted to bolt, but to Connie's relief he sat. "Okay, what's first?"

"The date," Connie said.

"What day could you come, Daddy?" Silver wiggled her way onto his lap. She smiled and patted his cheek.

"I'm invited?" He sounded bewildered.

"You have to be there," Silver said in all seriousness, "because the other kids at preschool think I made you up."

The pathos of those words wrenched Connie's heart. She glanced at Wade and saw that he, too, was moved.

"Uh, how about a week from today? Would that fit in your schedule?" Connie suggested.

Wade's head jerked up.

"Only a week?" He gulped.

"A whole week?" Silver mourned.

"You'll be so busy it will fly by," Connie promised Silver. "We have decorations to put up and party favors to make. Invitations to print. All kinds of stuff."

"Oh." For once Silver had nothing to say. But her big blue eyes brimmed with questions.

"What exactly are you planning to do at this party?" Wade licked his lips like a man in the desert craving water.

"Games, food, singing. All the things kids do at a party." Connie paused. "It is all right, isn't it?"

"A little late to ask me that," Wade mumbled, glancing at Silver's bent head meaningfully.

Connie studied the paper in front of her. Because if she looked up and met his stare, he'd see that she deliberately hadn't told him of her idea in case he vetoed it.

"Oh, never mind," he said, obviously disgruntled. "Plan away." He moved as if to rise.

"But I'm going to need your help," Connie blurted. It didn't take a genius to read his skepticism. "With a game," she said. "I can't do it alone."

"Why not?" he said, with one eyebrow tilted. "You've managed this far."

"I can't handle a whole treasure hunt on my own." It was an off-the-cuff response, the first thing she thought of, but Silver's gasp made Connie wish she hadn't said it aloud in case she couldn't deliver.

"The other kids would really like a treasure hunt, Daddy," she said, threading her arms around his neck. "So would I. Please?"

Wade held his little girl delicately, as if afraid she'd break. His fingers hovered over the gossamer silver hair as one would approach a butterfly and drew away just as quickly, fear chasing doubt as he eased out of Silver's exuberant embrace.

"Please, Daddy."

In that instant, Connie pitied Wade Abbott. He wanted to love Silver, she knew he did, though fear held him in its steely grip. Still, Silver was a powerful motivation to let go. With her blue eyes and adoring begging voice urging him to grant her request, most men would be putty in her hands. Poor Wade didn't stand a chance.

Then Connie forced away the rush of pity she was feeling. How stupid she was being. That was the whole point of this party—to get him more involved with Silver and help him shed this cloak of apprehension that clouded everything he did with his daughter.

Wade cleared his throat.

"Do you really need help?" he asked, a wary edge to his voice.

"Yes." Connie met his gaze head-on.

Time stretched taut like a wire between them until finally he nodded—once.

"Okay."

"Hooray for Daddy." Silver flung her arms around his neck and squeezed. She didn't seem to notice that Wade didn't return her hug, because she was too busy planning. She leaned forward and grabbed a sheet of paper. "Can you fix your old fort, Daddy? We could use it for the party. Grandma said you played there when you were little like me. She said you were a pirate. Will you be the pirate at my party?"

Wade's cheeks turned a vivid red.

"You were once a pirate?" Connie teased, wondering if this stiff, formal man would unbend enough to actually wear a costume.

"No, I—"

"I saw pictures, Daddy. You had a pirate hat and a sword, and you were standing on the fort. But Grandma won't let me go on it. She says its dil... dill..." Silver stopped, frowned.

"Dilapidated?" Wade finished and nodded. "It is." He glanced at Connie. "Nobody's used it since Danny—"

Once again that forlorn look washed across his face, and once again Connie's heart melted like butter on hot toast.

"Danny must have loved it, as you did. Most kids would," she said. "It would make a great center for the party," she coaxed. "We could hang balloons, play capture the flag, have our picnic near there."

Wade remained silent for a long time. Silver didn't notice. She was too busy drawing pictures of all the things she wanted to do at her party.

"I can plan something else, if you'd rather," Connie offered when Silver raced off to find some tape.

"Ha! I don't think she'd go for it," Wade retorted, but a half smile flirted with his lips. "She's locked on to this pirate idea now. There won't be any talking her out of using the fort."

"I certainly hope you'll make the place safe before you let anyone get on that derelict monstrosity, Wade." Amanda stood in the doorway, her face hard. "In fact, I think it should be torn down."

"No! We can't tear down the fort." Silver burst past her grandmother, her eyes brimming with tears.

"Don't be a silly sentimentalist," Amanda scoffed. "That old wreck is disgusting."

"It was my daddy's fort," Silver wailed. "He played there, and I want to, too."

There was no consoling Silver until Wade wiped away her tears and promised he'd have a look and see what could be done.

"Now no more tears, okay? Christmas is supposed to be a happy time."

"I promise, Daddy." Silver's bottom lip wobbled for an instant, but she finally regained control, favoring him with her big smile. "I love you, Daddy," she said. Then she gave his hard, chiseled cheek a kiss.

A moment later, she'd jumped down and was racing away to decide what toys she'd take out to the fort.

"She's going to get hurt, Wade. And it will be your fault. Again." Amanda glared at him before wheeling away.

Wade simply stood there, desolation robbing his handsome face of joy.

"Wow. Nothing easy about this party, is there?" Connie forced a laugh from her lips. She began gathering her supplies. "Don't worry about it. I'll plan something else."

"No." Wade sat down. "Silver wants to use the fort. Nothing wrong with that. It's the reason my father built it."

"He built it for you." Connie was amazed. Somehow, after seeing the stern portrait images in the upstairs hall, she'd never thought of Wade's father as anything but a very proper lawyer.

"He not only built it but he used to hide in it sometimes when my mother wanted him to clean out the garage or go to some society function." Wade's lips lifted in a brief grin. "He'd take a book, a jug of lemonade and a little tape player and hide up there for hours."

"You must miss him a lot," Connie offered.

Wade lifted his head and stared at her. After a moment, he nodded.

"Silver asks about her grandfather quite often. I think that's how she came to see pictures of you. She asked Amanda about your father. She's asked me, too, but I never know what to tell her." Connie held her breath, wondering if he'd understand that his daughter needed a sense of history to feel fully secure in this family.

"I could tell her lots of things." Wade glanced around. "How much he loved Christmas dinners in this room, for instance. I can still see him, sitting where you are and carving the turkey while everyone recited a verse from the nativity story.

He'd always invite a bunch of people for dinner so we were squeezed in like sardines."

"He sounds like a very generous, loving man," she said softly.

"He was." After a moment, Wade rose. "I miss him very much. And Danny. I wish Amanda understood that."

"Maybe you should tell her," Connie blurted, then wished she hadn't.

"Tell her what?" He scowled. "About my childhood?"

"About your memories. Share them with her."

"What good would that do?" he asked sourly.

"I don't know. Maybe make her feel less alone." She could tell he wasn't buying. "I've talked to Amanda a little," she offered.

"And?"

"I think she feels as if she's the only one grieving, as if she alone has to keep alive their memories." She paused to see if Wade was listening. "I think she's afraid to be happy because then she might forget about them."

Wade said nothing for a long time, and Connie wondered if she'd said too much. She cleared her throat and rose to leave. Wade moved to block her exit.

"Taking everyone under that motherly wing of yours, Connie?" He smiled to ease the hint of sarcasm in his words. Then he grasped her arm. "Come on," he urged.

"Where?" Connie eased out of his grip.

"To look at the fort. If the party is only a week away, we need to get busy."

Just like that?

Connie trailed behind Wade and stood outside, slightly bemused by his about-face. She waited silently in the warm sun as he tested the ramp, swung on the rope and generally sounded out the fort for defects.

"Needs a few tweaks," Wade said, grinning as he dusted off his pants. He jumped off the balcony and walked toward her, his face clear of all the strain she'd seen hovering there. "I'll have some stuff delivered tomorrow. Maybe David can give me a hand fixing it."

"I can help."

Wade's look expressed his doubts.

Connie laughed. "I built lots of things when I was on the farm. You might be surprised how good I am with a hammer."

"Thanks, but I doubt it will come to that. David is help enough."

"Okay." She didn't take offense. "But if you need an extra set of hands, I'm here."

"Thank you." He pulled out a pen and a piece of paper and began scribbling, muttering reminders to himself. He glanced up once. "Keep Silver away till it's finished, will you?"

"Of course."

"And Connie?"

"Yes?" She waited for the reprimand she knew was coming.

"Thanks for the other advice, too. I'll try talking to Amanda again."

"Good." Since she suddenly felt self-conscious with him, Connie hurried back inside to sketch out the rest of her plans. Then she and Silver hunkered over the computer in the office to figure out what kind of invitation they would make.

"What's going on now?" Wade asked some time later, from the doorway.

"I hope you don't mind," Connie said quickly. "David told me when he hired me that I could use the computer in your office."

"It's fine." He strolled over to take a look at their work. "Why aren't you printing them in color?"

"Can we?" Silver asked, eyes wide.

"I can't seem to set the printer," Connie explained.

"Like this." Wade touched a few buttons, and beautifully colored invitations spewed out in a graceful heap.

"Thank you." Connie showed Silver how to fold the papers in quarters.

"There's a new email," Wade said a moment later.

"I think that's mine." Connie reached for the mouse, her hand brushing his. Her first reflex action was to pull away guiltily, but Connie didn't do that. She wasn't willing to let him think for an instant that she was harboring thoughts like that other nanny.

Instead, she waited for Wade to remove his hand then clicked on the icon. The message filled the screen.

"Oh."

"Something good?" Wade asked. He'd moved to stand in front of the desk to give her privacy.

"Something very good. I've found another man who says he knew my father. He's agreed to meet me." Connie hit print, watched the email message appear then folded it and tucked it in her pocket.

"Are you 'cited?" Silver wanted to know. "Connie's been looking for her daddy for a long time," she explained to her father.

"Ah." Wade watched Connie with those intense brown eyes but said nothing more.

"I know my dad probably won't want to see me after this many years," Connie said, cheeks hot with embarrassment at displaying her eagerness to speak to this man. She sounded needy in her own ears. "But I want to talk to him."

"Of course." Wade didn't look convinced.

"There are questions—things I'd like to know," she burbled wondering why she was trying to justify herself.

"I'm sure. When does this man want to meet you?" Wade asked. He glanced at Silver for an instant.

In that look, Connie saw speculation, as if he'd just realized that many of Silver's questions about her grandfather would be like the ones Connie wanted to ask her dad. Connie had a lot of questions—most of all, why he'd left her.

"He says Sunday, tomorrow night," she said. "He'll be at the evening service at the drop-in center. I'll meet him before it starts."

Silver tugged on Connie's hand, bored with the conversation. "Can I give Grandma a paper about the party?"

"Can you print your name on it yourself?"

"Of course," Silver said, her eyes wide as if scandalized by the very idea that she couldn't write her own name. To prove it, she carefully scribed the letters and added a lopsided bell with an odd-shaped clapper.

"Very nice." Connie smiled and showed her how to fold it. "She'll be the very first one to get an invitation." She watched the little girl scamper happily away.

"Um, that may not have been the best idea," Wade murmured.

"Because?"

His brown eyes brimmed with sad memories. Connie wanted to know what had caused them.

"My father and Danny were killed the week before Christmas," Wade said, his voice flat. "Amanda doesn't really celebrate."

"Oh, dear." Connie's heart flooded with sympathy for the poor woman, but what could she do now? "You should have said something earlier."

"I would have, if you'd asked me."

"I'm sorry," she said. And she was. The last thing this family needed was more grief.

Wade studied her for a long moment.

"Is something wrong?" She shifted uncomfortably under his stare.

"Christmas is very important to you, isn't it?" he said.

"Yes."

"Care to tell me why?" He sat down in one of the leather tufted armchairs and waited.

What could she tell him? That at twenty-two she still dreamed of an answer to the same Christmas prayer she'd prayed for the past eleven years—that her father would appear and tell her he loved her, that leaving her had been a mistake? How silly.

"I'm sorry," he said, moving as if to rise. "I'm prying."

"No, you're not. It's a valid question." She waved him back into his seat as she struggled to explain.

"My birth mother was the one who started it. She loved Christmas, and she made it a joy for everyone around her. We lived in a little town, and I can still remember sitting on the toboggan on Christmas Eve while she pulled me across town. Packed all around me were gifts—pots of jam, tins of shortbread, boxes of fudge."

"You're making me hungry," he said with a smile.

"My parents owned a hardware store. We lived above it. On Christmas Eve, when the last customer was gone, their gift perfectly wrapped, my parents would close up shop. Then Mom would serve us supper. After the dishes were done, Dad would disappear to wrap his gifts. He always had some prank planned."

"Sounds like quite a character."

"He was. Is," she corrected herself. "Mom and I would load up the sleigh and deliver gifts she'd chosen, little things for folks she'd heard about who needed some Christmas cheer."

"She walked?"

"It was a very small town. No need to drive." Connie smiled. "She never seemed to feel the cold—nor did I. The nights were so frigid that the snow crackled under our feet. But the sky was always spectacular, stars glittering everywhere. It didn't take much for me to imagine shepherds with their sheep in the fields or the angels appearing in that dark sky, a brilliant white heavenly host."

"Bethlehem didn't have snow, or cold," Wade corrected, his voice amused.

"Didn't matter to me. The air was so crisp and still, hushed and expectant. I always half wondered if we'd turn a corner and happen upon the manger and Mary with her baby." Memories engulfed her and she had to stop and compose herself. "We'd stop at each house, and Mom would hand over whichever treat she'd prepared especially for them and wish them a Merry Christmas. Then we'd go on to the next place."

"Didn't they invite you in?" he asked.

"Oh, yes, but Mom never stopped. She had so many things to deliver. And probably gifts at home to finish. She always made Christmas gifts for Dad and me." Connie laughed as past scenes cascaded through her mind. "One year I got a big green frog that was a pajama bag. It sat on my bed. I was Silver's age, and I was so proud of it."

"Your mother left quite a legacy."

"Yes," Connie agreed. "She died when I was eight."

"I'm sorry."

"Dad was never quite the same after that. But he always tried hard to make our Christmases special. That's why I couldn't understand why—"

"You don't have to tell me," Wade said softly.

"One day I was home and the next I was alone. Why? That's what I don't understand." Connie gulped down the tears, refusing to cry in front of him. But one seeped out and dribbled down her chin anyway.

"Connie…" The empathy in his low voice was her undoing.

"I should be past this," she said fiercely, angry that so many years had passed and yet those same old feelings of abandonment still clung to her inner child.

"I don't suppose it's all that easy to get over childhood trauma." Wade's quiet voice was etched in unspoken pain. "For anyone."

Sensitive to his anguish, Connie let a few moments pass before she rose and gathered the invitations.

"Anyway, I try to keep Christmas as my mother did, to honor her memory and to honor her faith in God's love for us. That's why it's so important to me." *And because I'm still a stupid kid who daydreams that one day her dad will tell her he wants her, that he loves her.*

Wade said nothing when she hurried away.

He was probably more embarrassed by her display of emotion than by the last nanny's pleas for affection.

But at least he'd promised to help with Silver's party.

Chapter Five

As Wade walked downstairs on Sunday night, the hall clock chimed seven o'clock.

"Going out?" Connie spared him a quick look as she buttoned her bright red sweater.

She wore red a lot, Wade had noticed. And no wonder—it did great things for her dark hair and that creamy porcelain skin.

"I have a date—with a book on South American architecture," he said. "Where are you off to?" Wade didn't want to sound too prying. After all, it was none of his business what the nanny did on her night off.

"I'm going to speak with the man who knew my father, the one who sent the email."

"Oh, yes." He frowned. The address of the drop-in center where Connie was meeting her informant was in an unsavory area of town. Though he didn't like the thought of her traveling there alone after dark, and returning even later, especially after David had told him of two violent incidents mere days earlier, he could hardly forbid her.

As if on cue, Silver bounded down the stairs, blue eyes shining. Wade couldn't suppress the rush of pride that flooded him, but he quickly called himself a fool. Why should he feel pride? Silver wasn't really his daughter. He was only pretending she was.

"Daddy! Can we go?"

"Go where?" Wade asked as Connie checked her watch and favored him with a "nanny" look that said, 'This child should soon be tucked into her bed."

"To look at the Christmas lights," Silver explained, bouncing from one foot to the other, the bells on her shoes jingling a merry tune. "Cora and I saw it on TV. There's a whole bunch of houses with pretty lights. Can we go, Daddy? Please?"

What red-blooded man could resist those wide baby blue eyes and that beseeching tone? Not Wade. He stuffed aside thoughts of his book and pulled his jacket out of the closet.

"I guess so. But you need to bring a warm sweater."

"Woo hoo," Silver whooped as she raced back to her room.

Connie's wide-eyed stare unnerved him.

"What? You can hardly object," he muttered.

"We both know you've been scheming nonstop to get me to spend more time with her."

"Hardly scheming," she protested. A faint pink tinge colored her flawless skin. "And I certainly am not objecting. I'm just—"

"What? Surprised?"

"Glad." Her wide eyes and expressive face gave away her emotions. At the moment, Connie's face blazed with joy. For him? "She's going to love it. It will be a memory she'll treasure."

"Maybe." He wondered how many of those they'd have before his guilt completely overwhelmed him and he was forced to find Silver's real family.

"I'm ready, Daddy."

Wade pushed away the ugly thoughts. Later, he promised himself. He'd think it through later. For now he was going to grab this smidgen of happiness which life had offered.

"Are you three all going out?" Amanda stood at the top of the stairs, frowning down at them.

"Daddy and I are going to see Christmas lights." Silver clapped her hands. "Why don't you come with us, Grandma? And Connie. Then you could see the lights, too."

Wade had been struggling to come up with a way to open a discussion with his stepmother. Was this it?

"Interested, Amanda? It might be fun." He doubted she'd agree. For one thing, she was mad at him again because he'd circumvented another of her attempts to have the board rescind his decision to hire two new associates.

But Silver didn't know that. She dashed up the stairs and grabbed Amanda's hands, tugging on them.

"Come on, Grandma. It will be fun. They have rides, too—wagons with real horses!" Silver's voice kept rising.

"You're going to Winterhaven?" Amanda asked very quietly.

"Yes." Wade lifted his chin. "Dad used to take me there. I thought I'd do the same for Silver."

"He took D-Danny, too."

"I remember. It was their tradition. Maybe you could tell Silver about them." Wade held his breath and waited.

Amanda's face crumpled. She opened her mouth to say something more, but after a quick glance at Silver, she gave her head a slight shake.

"Don't let *her* get hurt" was all she managed before she turned around and rushed away.

A truckload of guilt weighed heavily on his shoulders even though Wade knew he hadn't been to blame in either Danny's or his father's deaths. It was done, over. Why couldn't she let it go?

Silver walked slowly downstairs and stopped in front of him.

"Why is Grandma sad, Daddy?" she asked. "Did I do something bad?"

"No, Silver. You didn't do anything wrong." Guilt wasn't going to become her constant companion, not if he could help it.

"Then why is she sad?"

Wade's heart squeezed tight at the misery washing through the child's previously sparkling blue eyes. He squatted down in front of her and cupped her face in his palms.

"Some very special people who meant a lot to Grandma died near Christmas. She gets sad remembering, that's all. You didn't do anything."

"But maybe if she came with us she'd be happy for a while," Silver said.

"Maybe she would. But Grandma isn't ready to do that." Silver looked confused, and Wade wasn't sure how to explain. "She needs time," he added, but that didn't help so he looked to Connie for assistance.

True to form, Connie was ready for the challenge.

"Remember when you didn't want to go near the puppets at storytime, Silver?" she asked, crouching down next to Wade.

The little girl nodded.

"I tried to tell you that they were fun and that you'd like listening to their stories, didn't I?"

"Yes." Silver frowned.

"But you wouldn't go until you were ready, would you?" Connie looked at him as if asking permission to continue.

Wade nodded. She was so much better at this than he.

"But then I got ready," Silver said proudly. "I like the puppets."

"Now you do. But you found out you liked them when you were ready, not because I told you that you would." Connie smoothed the static-laden hair that danced around Silver's head like a halo. "That's how it is with your grandmother, honey. When she's ready, she'll let God shine the light of Christmas into her heart, and it will push her sadness away."

"It will?" Silver's eyes widened.

"Yes. Because that's what Christmas is all about," Connie explained. "Christmas happened because God sent His love to heal us."

"Oh." Silver stood silent, thinking about it. "It's kind of like my bells, isn't it?"

"Is it?" Wade asked. "How?"

"When my bells ring, people always smile."

She was so smart, this precious little girl.

"Yes, they sure do." Wade grinned. He stretched to his full height. "So would you like to come with us?" he said, looking at Connie. "We could stop by where you're going, wait for you, and then go on to Winterhaven, if you'd like to come."

"I might be a while," she said. She stood, but her gaze remained on Silver. "We could be late coming home."

So she thought of his place as home. That should worry him. Wade had never wanted the other nanny to think like that. But Connie was different. She didn't take liberties. She was focused on her job—Silver. Not him.

"Couldn't Silver handle one late night?" Wade asked. "I don't want to wreck your schedule, but if I recall correctly, she has no pressing engagement for tomorrow morning." He waited for Connie's assent, knowing Silver was watching them with bated breath.

Apparently Connie also realized that little pitchers had big ears.

"Well," she mused in a thoughtful tone, "I don't know. Sometimes when Silver doesn't get enough sleep, she gets, well—"

"I won't be grumpy, Connie. I promise." Her blue eyes darted from one to the other. "And I'll go to bed early tomorrow night."

"Wow, you must really want to go." Connie chuckled. "Okay, for one night I don't think it will hurt. But since we have our Sunday school practice tomorrow afternoon, maybe you can have a nap before it."

"Babies have naps," Silver said, her voice oozing scorn. Then she looked at him.

Wade lifted one eyebrow but said nothing. Silver sighed.

"Okay," she agreed at last. "A nap *if* I'm tired."

"Then let's go." He told Cora they were leaving, and she handed him a bag to drop off at Winterhaven. "I'll explain later," he told Connie. When Wade had stored it in the trunk, he opened the door and waited for Connie and Silver to climb in. Suddenly, he was feeling a bit of Silver's excitement.

The center was located in a part of town Wade hadn't visited in years. It made him glad he'd driven Connie here and doubly glad he could ensure she'd leave safely. At least, it would be a good idea, if his car was still in one piece when they left.

Inside the hall, a number of people sat waiting for the Sunday evening service to begin while others finished dinner. Wade and Silver took a seat in the back of the room as Connie approached the director at the front. After a brief conversation, he led her to a grizzled, whiskered man seated in a wheelchair. Connie held out the note; the man nodded and began to speak.

Wade was too far away to hear the conversation. He grabbed a brochure off a nearby table and began to read about New Horizons, the center where Connie had come to find her father. He didn't get far.

"Daddy?" Silver edged a little closer to him, her voice whisper soft. "What is this place?"

"Um." How should he phrase this?

"Those people look sad. Did somebody hurt them, Daddy?"

"I don't think so." Wade scanned the information quickly. "New Horizons is for people to come and get help. I guess some of them don't have homes to go to." He tried to put the health care crisis into terms she'd understand. "Maybe they spent all their money trying to get better. Anyway, they come here to eat, go on the computers to look for jobs," he added, having just read that, "and to meet with people to talk about their feelings."

"Oh." Clearly mystified, Silver didn't ask any more, and Wade didn't volunteer. After a few moments, she climbed onto his knee and held his hand with both of hers.

But when a little boy arrived with a woman pushing his wheelchair, Silver perked up. She watched the mother serve her child some food. The boy managed, with the awkward grace of his unbandaged hand, to feed himself. When his mother finished her meal and began to speak to him, he listened intently then nodded his head and watched her walk across the room.

"Can I go talk to him, Daddy?"

Wade hesitated. What if Silver asked the wrong question and hurt the disabled boy's feelings? But Silver was usually very careful of others' feelings. He decided to take the risk.

"Be polite" was the best fatherly advice he could think of. What a failure he was at this parenting business. Far better to let Connie handle it.

"Okay." Silver hopped off his knee and tinkled her way across the room to the boy.

Being careful not to look too curious and invade Silver's line of sight, Wade shifted to a seat a few feet behind the pair, prepared to interrupt if the scowling boy hurt his baby.

How pathetic was he? Afraid to embrace fatherhood completely, yet acting like a besotted daddy ready to protect his kid from everything.

He glanced up and found Connie's gaze on him. It slid to Silver and the boy and then back to him. She smiled, and Wade knew he'd been caught out in his pretend fatherly role. But he stayed where he was anyway. Just in case.

"Hi. My name is Silver."

"So?" The boy continued eating as if she wasn't there.

Wade told himself to ignore the rudeness and stay cool.

"So what's your name?" Silver climbed into the chair beside his wheelchair and waited.

"Kris." Other than the single word, the boy ignored her.

"Do you live here, Kris?"

Wade held his breath when the boy glared at her.

"Nobody *lives* here, dummy."

"Oh." Unabashed, Silver swung her feet, bells faintly tinkling. "What do you want for Christmas?"

"A million bucks."

The kid had a smart lip, and Wade was getting tired of it. But Silver hadn't given up, and Wade was loathe to drag her away when Connie didn't seem ready to leave.

"I want God to help my daddy love me," Silver told him. "And a dollhouse."

Whatever they said next flew right over Wade's head.

I want God to help my daddy love me.

His gut clenched as if he'd been sucker punched by one of the gangs he was quite sure ran this side of town. The words spun around his brain like a whirling dervish, deeper and deeper. Every syllable a condemnation.

Why couldn't he say the words? He'd give up his life if it would keep this child safe. But he couldn't force the words, "I love you, Silver," through his lips. And that was hurting her—something he did not want to do.

What was wrong with him?

Lots. But in his deepest heart, Wade knew that it was better that he didn't say those words. If he told her that, how could he ever bear to let her go?

Kris's mother began to play a battered piano,

choosing old familiar carols. The haunting notes lent a soothing atmosphere to the room, and voices dropped to a whisper. A young girl washing dishes in the kitchen began to sing along. Others soon joined her.

Of course they sang about love, the kind of love that had nothing to do with rights or deserving. The kind of love that was exemplified by the greatest gift of all.

And all Wade wanted to do was leave.

"Is everything okay?" Connie slid into the seat next to his, a slight frown marring the perfection of her pretty face.

"Did you find out what you need to?" he asked, ignoring her question.

"All I could, for now." She kept studying him, unnerving him with that steady scrutiny that asked questions Wade didn't want to answer.

"Then let's go. After all, we don't want Silver to stay up too late." It was a cop out, and Wade knew she knew it.

Connie simply rose and waited while he moved toward Silver.

"Time to go, kiddo."

"Okay. This is Kris. That's his mom playing the piano," Silver explained. "Isn't she pretty?"

"Very." He glanced at the woman and frowned. At this angle she looked oddly familiar. "What's your mom's name, son?"

The kid looked as if he'd like to tell Wade that he wasn't his son. But he restrained the urge and muttered, "Klara."

"Klara Kramer?" Wade asked in surprise.

"Kramer was my grandparents' name," the boy said. "They died."

"My grandpa died, too," Silver said. "But it was before I was borned." She tilted her head up to look at Wade. "Kris's dad died. His mom hasn't got a job. They come here lots so she can find one."

Silver babbled away, but Wade lost the rest of what she said. Klara Kramer was a well-known draftswoman. Or she had been.

"Wade?" Connie touched his arm. "Is anything wrong?"

"No." Wade took one last look at the woman at the piano. An idea began taking shape in his brain.

"Daddy?" Silver tugged on his arm.

"We should go now, Silver." He'd have to think about this later. "You better say goodbye."

"Okay. But can we come again, Daddy?"

"We'll see," he said, employing the age-old non-committal response his own father had often used on him.

"Kris was telling me about his school. It sounds so fun." Silver bid the boy a sweet goodbye then skipped between him and Connie toward the door. "I can hardly wait to go to real school."

Once in the car, Connie made sure Silver was buckled in. She would have sat in the back beside her, but Silver insisted she wanted Connie to sit in the front seat.

"In case I get tired," she said.

Surprised, Wade checked his rearview mirror. Silver admitting to tiredness? Not hardly. But she was happily humming to herself, glancing from left to right as if checking the view, so he let it go. Anyway, he wanted to find out what Connie had learned about her father. It seemed important to know how her search was going, though Wade didn't understand why that should matter to him.

But he didn't press her because one, it was none of his business, and two, he wasn't sure if Silver should hear it or not. So instead, he answered Connie's questions about the festival of lights.

"A Tucson resident named CB Richards was the founder of Winterhaven Water and Development Company. He visited Beverly Hills in the 1930s, and after seeing their light displays, he wanted to create the same at home. He purchased the first set of lights in 1949 and donated them to the community. After that, he bought allepo pines from a local nursery that was going out of business and had them planted at regular intervals where he also had electrical connections hooked up."

"Quite a farsighted thinker," Connie murmured.

"Oh, yes. He personally judged the first festival

contests where the winner was awarded one hundred dollars," Wade explained, dredging up details his father had told him. He'd almost forgotten his father's love of this festival. "Years later, after Richards moved to San Diego, he continued to visit Winterhaven for the festival. The contest has run every year, except for once in the 1970s during an energy crisis when residents voted to stay dark."

"Is there an admission fee?" she wondered.

"No. You're supposed to bring nonperishable food or donations, which go to the local food bank." Wade pointed. "See the food bank volunteers stationed at the entrances? They collect donations."

"I'm not carrying much cash," Connie murmured, pulling her wallet from her purse. "But I do want to contribute."

"I have some stuff Cora sent along," Wade told her, but Connie insisted on handing the volunteer money while he and Silver toted their gifts of food to the huge box wrapped with a red bow.

"Thank you and enjoy," the volunteers said.

"It's massive," Connie whispered peering out the windshield. "Look at those houses!"

"Stop, Daddy. I want to see."

"We're going to see it all, Silver, after I park. This isn't a drive-thru night, so we can't go in the car. We'll take a carriage instead. This spot looks good." He parked and shut off the engine. "We'll wait over there for our ride to come."

Wade locked the car then retrieved the blanket he'd stowed in the trunk.

"In case it gets cool," he told Connie.

"Wow, you really think ahead." She grinned.

Wade shrugged.

"I always carry it. Everyone thinks of the desert as hot. And it is, in the summer. But the nights can get really cool, especially in winter." He motioned. "Hence the fire."

He led them to a group of people sitting on hay bales around a campfire. Some chattered, and some were silently staring into the flames. In the background, a group sang carols. Wade heard the clop of horses' hooves approaching and pointed them out to Silver.

"Are those our horsies, Daddy?" She squeezed his hand tight, her excitement palpable.

"I don't know. We'll have to see if they have room."

"You shouldn't have waited for me," Connie said, her forehead pleated in a frown. "I delayed you."

"It's no big deal. We'll take whatever transport is available. Sunday night is popular, but we're early in the season."

"Couldn't we walk?" Connie asked, darting a glance at the glittering arrays twinkling ahead.

"Yes, there are many people who walk it. You might want to do that another night," Wade said, inclining his head toward Silver.

Connie nodded her understanding.

As it happened, the hayride wagons bulged with kids' groups who'd reserved them. But Wade saw a carriage standing empty, off to one side.

"Stay here," he told Connie. "I'll be right back."

The driver's clients were over half an hour late, so he readily agreed to Wade's terms and pulled his horses into the lineup.

"This one's ours," Wade said, smiling as Silver's eyes swelled.

"Your horses are lovely," Connie said. She patted the neck of the nearest animal and whispered something. It whinnied and threw back its head. "What a pretty girl," she murmured as she brushed its nose.

Wade felt Silver's hand creep into his and squeeze very tight.

"Don't be afraid," he told her as he lifted her into his arms.

"Mistletoe and Holly are special horses," the driver told her as he dismounted. "They love showing off our fancy lights. They especially love little girls." He pulled an apple out of his carriage. "Would you like to feed them, missy?"

"Horses eat apples?" Silver asked, her voice shocked.

"They love them. Here." He placed the apple in her hand. Quick as a flash, the horse nearest her leaned over and carefully plucked the apple from her hand. After thoroughly chewing it, he bent and rubbed his ear against Silver's shoulder.

"He touched me," the little girl squealed in delight. Very slowly, with great precision, she reached out and touched a finger to the horse's nose. "Which one is he?"

"She. That's Holly. She can sneak a carrot out of your pocket if you're not looking." The driver gave her another apple for Mistletoe.

As Wade walked around to the other side, still holding Silver, he caught Connie studying them. For a moment, he thought he saw a tear glimmer on the end of her lashes but decided it was the light when Silver begged him to let her down. When she'd fed the other horse her apple, they all climbed aboard the carriage, Silver seated between him and Connie, wiggling constantly to see everything.

They'd only progressed about two blocks when the driver stopped and turned around.

"Would the little girl like to sit up here and help me drive the horses?"

"I don't think—" Wade began as fear gripped his throat.

Silver drowned him out.

"Please, Daddy? Please can I? I'll be very good. I won't scare them or anything."

"There's a seat 'specially made for kids up here," the driver told them. "It has a seat belt with a special locking mechanism so kids can't wiggle out. It's very safe."

Silver kept begging. Even Connie added her encouragement. But Wade couldn't get rid of his dread. What if something happened? What if the carriage tipped or the horses stumbled? He glanced at Connie. She shifted Silver so she could lean near him.

"Sometimes you just have to let go and trust God to take care of the thing you love most," she whispered.

Trust God?

He'd trusted God—and his father and Danny had died.

He'd trusted God with Bella and—

"Please, Daddy?" Silver's pink nose was an inch from his. Then she pressed her soft, sweet lips against his cheek. "Please?"

Wade squeezed his eyes closed, sucked in a breath of courage and sighed.

"Let me see that seat," he said.

A short while later, they were again clopping down the street. Silver sat still as a mouse in her seat in front, her eyes huge as she divided her attention between the lights and the horses. Wade sat forward in his seat. Though no one could tell, he had a firm hold on Silver's sweater.

Correction—Connie could tell. But there was understanding in her gray eyes when she smiled at him. As if she knew how very afraid he was of losing the last thing he had left, the thing that gave his world meaning, the child he would one day lose.

"She's fine, Wade. Silver's perfectly fine." Connie's sotto-voiced words carried on the night zephyr and somehow helped him relax. "'For I, the Lord your God, will hold your right hand, saying unto you, Fear not, I will help you.'" She smiled. "That's Isaiah 41:13, my foster mother's favorite verse. You might want to look it up."

He decided he might just do that, if it would help him gain the assurance that Connie had.

"This house is my special favorite," the driver said, turning so they could all hear him. "It seems the most Christmassy to me."

Wade agreed.

The perfectly lit scene showcased a figure—a father beside his fireplace, a child on his knee as he read from a big book while the flames flickered merrily beside him. Words were spelled out on the lawn.

Be not afraid. I bring you good tidings of great joy.

An angel hovered over the scene.

"An angel, Daddy. Just like I'm going to be."

Not yet, God, Wade's heart begged. *Not for a long, long time. I promise I'll do the right thing for Silver. I'll give her up. Only don't let her be hurt.*

The rest of the ride through Winterhaven seemed long to Wade. He was glad when they returned home, glad when he finally hugged Silver good-night, glad when she left with Connie and he was alone.

Then and only then did he retreat to his study. He pulled out his Bible and found the words Connie had quoted. *Fear not, I will help you.*

He was going to need help, because tonight had finally hammered home the truth. It was time to stop pretending he was a father and make things right for Silver.

He flicked on his computer to begin the search for his daughter's real family.

Chapter Six

The telephone call Connie had just received about her father made no sense. He couldn't be dead.

But she had no time to mull it over. With Silver's party in full swing, it took every ounce of Connie's ingenuity to keep the children busy and involved, especially since Wade had not yet appeared.

"He's probably too busy with a new girlfriend to bother with Silver," Amanda offered in a snarky tone as she popped one of the balloons Connie had painstakingly hung around the newly refurbished fort.

"He wasn't too busy to get this fort fixed up," Connie replied and then wished she hadn't stooped to arguing with Wade's stepmother.

"Of course he did. Covering his liabilities," Amanda sneered. She shrugged. "He's got to protect himself."

The wail of a child who'd just skinned his

knee cut across her words. Connie's frustration peaked.

"Amanda, can't you, just once, say something nice about the man?"

"He isn't here." Amanda pouted. "I think that's nice."

"Not what I meant and you know it." Now a second child was wailing. "Is it possible that you could be a help today instead of a hindrance?" Connie demanded, exasperated by the woman's negativity. Without waiting for an answer, she hurried away to soothe and treat the wounded limb.

Even with Hornby, Cora and cranky Amanda's help, Connie had her hands full with the party. Not the least because of Silver's constant question.

"Is Daddy here yet?"

Every time Silver received a negative answer, her face dropped a little more. It became harder to engage her in any activity. When tears appeared, Connie's tolerance for the absentee father evaporated.

"Okay, children. It's time for our lunch. Everyone look for your name at the table." While they raced around, Connie grabbed the phone, hid behind a shrub and dialed Wade's office. "I need to speak to him immediately," she told his secretary.

"I'm sorry, Mr. Abbot is unavailable—"

"Make him available," Connie said. "This is urgent."

"Just a moment."

Seconds later, Wade's voice came on the line.

"Yes, Connie?"

"There's a little girl here whom you promised would see you at her party," she snapped. "It's half over, and she's still waiting."

"I'm very busy—" he began.

Too irritated for caution, Connie spoke from her heart.

"You're too chicken," she said bitterly. "I should have known you'd wimp out on your daughter. It's getting easier, isn't it? Because you've done it for so long. Forget it." She hung up on Wade's silence.

"Was that Daddy?" Silver asked, hope barely sparking in her sad blue eyes.

"Yes, it was. He's trying to get here, sweetheart." Which was true, Connie reasoned. Wade was fighting an internal battle to rid himself of his fears and embrace Silver. And she was probably out of a job. "Let's eat our hot dogs."

Connie left the other adults in charge while she quickly hid the treasure hunt items. As she did, she prayed nonstop that Wade would show up before she had to start the game, because when it was finished, the kids would go home.

"Okay, it's time for our Christmas birthday cake," she said when the hot dog stack had diminished to almost nothing.

"It's not my birthday," Silver said, blinking her surprise.

"No. Christmas is Jesus' birthday. So I thought we should have a cake." Connie motioned to Cora who emerged proudly bearing a beautifully iced cake with red and green candles burning around a baby lying in a manger. In the corner of the cake, an angel hovered.

"An angel, just like I'm going to be," Silver breathed.

Each child stared in wonder as Cora set the huge cake on the table. Minutes later, they eagerly joined in singing "Happy Birthday." Everyone blew on the candles. Then Cora cut the cake, Hornby handed it around and the adults watched it being devoured. After sticky fingers had been washed, Wade was still not present.

She could delay no longer. Connie explained the rules of the treasure hunt.

"Okay, there are four leaders. Cora, Hornby, Amanda and—"

"And me," said a low voice behind her.

Thank You, God.

"Daddy!" Silver raced up to him and squeezed his legs. Then she turned to a little boy named Reggie, who'd been bugging her all afternoon. "See, I do so have a daddy," she said.

Wade's face offered visible proof of how deeply those words affected him. Connie tried to express her appreciation with her eyes but remained silent. While Wade worked at disguising his emotions, she explained to the children how the game would work.

"Everything you need is in the yard," she said. "You don't have to look inside the house at all. But you do have to work as teams. Your leader will give you a clue. When you find the answer, you all bring it back and put it in your bucket. Then your leader will tell you the next clue. Okay?"

There were many questions, of course, but eventually Wade drew names and the children were divided into their teams. Connie sent each leader to one corner of the yard. Then the fun began. Silver and Reggie, who'd been her nemesis, were both on Wade's team, which meant Wade spent several moments settling arguments between them. Finally they reached a compromise, Connie blew the whistle and the game began. The children dashed about the yard, laughing, cheering and generally causing mayhem.

"This is what was so important for me to attend?" Wade grumbled when Connie paused to check his team's efforts.

"This is what it's all about," she told him with a grin. "Besides, you promised Silver you'd be here."

"I *was* coming," he claimed, but he quickly gave up that argument when she simply stared at him.

The completion of the game was a close finish, which Connie declared a four-way tie.

"That's not fair," Silver complained. "We got all our things before the others did. We're the only winners."

"Are you sure?" Connie asked each team leader to empty their contents on the table. The children gathered around, watching as she chose one thing from each team's pile.

"She's making a kite," one child exclaimed.

"Yes, I am," Connie agreed. "But I couldn't make it unless everyone finished. I need all the parts. That's why you're all winners, because you each found something we need. It doesn't matter who finished first, does it?"

Heads nodded their agreement.

"So we had to work together to get what we all need to make a kite," Reggie mused, eyes wide at her creation.

"Exactly." Connie smiled.

Cooperation blossomed as the children happily helped each other form the struts and wings on the simple box kites. Then they tried to get the contraptions airborne on the afternoon's light teasing winds.

"Very clever," Wade murmured from behind her.

"Thank you, but I got the idea off the internet."

"You use the internet a lot, don't you?" he asked.

"Why not?" Sensing a rebuke, Connie frowned. "It's a good resource."

"I guess." The doorbell rang, and he went to answer it.

Amanda disappeared the moment the game was over, so Wade and Silver greeted the parents and sent the children off with loot bags while Connie helped Cora and Hornby clear the mess. When the cleanup was finished, she thanked them for their help. Order was completely restored to the yard by the time Wade and Silver returned, except for a few wayward balloons on the fort. Connie decided to leave them when Silver flung her arms around her.

"Thank you for the bestest party in the whole world."

"You're welcome, sweetie." Connie hugged her tightly, set her down and watched the little girl turn to her father.

"Thank you for coming, Daddy. Reggie said he won't tease me about my daddy anymore."

"Oh?" Wade frowned. "Why not?"

"'Cause now he knows you're real." Smiling, Silver carried her kite across the yard and sat down on a sunny patch of grass to play with it.

Wade turned to leave, but Connie stopped

him. His eyes followed her hand, and she self-consciously let it drop away from his arm.

"I owe you an apology."

"Because?" He looked puzzled, not angry.

"I shouldn't have said what I did on the phone. It was rude and not my place."

Wade kept watching her. Growing more uncomfortable by the second, Connie shifted under his stare and kept her head downcast, eyes on the ground. A moment later, she heard a burst of laughter and glanced up.

"That apology must have cost you dearly," he chuckled.

"Well, I didn't expect you to laugh at me," she said, indignant that he would mock her.

"I'm not. Well, not really," Wade said, still grinning. "Connie, do you think I don't know that where Silver is concerned you're like a mother bear protecting her cub from anyone who would hurt her?"

"That's my job." Connie met his gaze and held it, fully aware of the electricity sizzling between them and the moment their interaction turned personal.

Wade knew it, too. His smile dropped away, leaving only his dark brown eyes intently peering into hers, searching for—something.

"That is what you hired me to do, isn't it?" she said quietly. When he didn't speak, she decided to tell him everything that lay on her heart. "Not that I think you'd deliberately hurt Silver."

"Thank you for that at least." He studied her then finally asked, "What *do* you think?"

"That you're afraid of the power she has over you," Connie said boldly. His eyes widened at the impact of her words, but she couldn't stop. "You're afraid that if you let yourself love her too much, you won't be able to let her go. And you're determined to let her go. Aren't you?"

Wade shifted, glancing over one shoulder to see if Silver was listening. But the little girl, worn out by the afternoon's events, had curled up in a chair and was now fast asleep.

"Why are you so afraid?" It was the one thing Connie didn't understand.

"I'm not her father," he said very quietly, anger coloring the edges of his voice. "She belongs with her true family."

"Who is that?"

"I don't know—yet," he admitted. "But I'll find them."

"And how will they be her true family?" Connie asked, keeping her voice low enough that even if Silver awakened, she wouldn't be able to hear. "Does she know any of them as she knows you, has known you all her life?"

"She'll learn to know them, to love them." His body shifted, his shoulders hunched forward in a defensive state, though he was probably unaware of it. "Children are adaptable."

"Silver has a great capacity for love, yes," Connie agreed. "But that also leaves her terribly vulnerable to being hurt by those she cares most about. You," she added.

"I won't ever hurt her" was Wade's fierce response. Then his voice altered, evidencing his frustration. "I'll just tell her that I'm not really her father, that there was a mistake."

"In what world would that make it better for Silver?" Disgust, frustration and anger spilled together and spurted inside Connie's heart like a geyser of pure acid. "To Silver you are her father. To be rejected—"

"I'm not rejecting her!" Wade spat out angrily.

Connie grasped his arm and drew him to the far side of the yard, so they wouldn't disturb the child. Wade followed her lead, but he clearly was not happy.

"You insist on attributing the worst possible motives to me. I don't *want* to send her to someone else," he insisted.

"Don't you?" Connie wasn't ready to let him off the hook. "Wouldn't that make it easier for you?"

"No!" He glared at her. "How could that be easier?"

"Because you wouldn't have to risk losing her once you'd let yourself love her."

"I—" The words seemed to shock him into silence. Or else Wade was so furious that he couldn't speak. Either way, he let his angry gaze do the talking.

"I know you think it's none of my business, but I care about her."

"It *is* none of your business," Wade gritted.

"It is because Silver trusts me. I don't want to see her get hurt." She studied him for a moment. "My former fiancé was a lot like you."

"Really? The lawyer?" He was deliberately goading her now.

Connie ignored his tone.

"Yes."

"How?" Wade challenged.

"He said all the right things, did all the right things. He seemed like he would be the perfect husband, just like you seem the perfect father. You give Silver lovely gifts, nice clothes, expensive schooling."

"What's wrong with that?"

"Nothing." She wouldn't release his gaze from hers.

"Then?" Wade sounded totally exasperated.

"My fiancé offered material things, too. A beautiful diamond ring, a lovely home, fancy places we were supposed to travel to." She smiled at him.

"Except the real man showed himself, and his pretend love was nothing but a sham. It became obvious that he never really loved me at all."

"I don't think the comparison is valid, but do go on," Wade ordered tersely.

"His concern that I not wear myself out caring for Billy?" She shook her head. "That was really concern that he wouldn't get all my attention and that I wouldn't be there, free to do whatever he wanted when he wanted."

"You make him sound selfish." Wade crossed his arms over his chest.

"I don't make him sound that way. He was." Connie shrugged. "His loss, because what he couldn't see was that Billy would have enriched his life far beyond the precious few moments he cost. He would have gained infinitely more if he'd stopped being afraid."

"So I'm afraid?"

Connie met his gaze and nodded.

"Of what?" he demanded.

"That you might get hurt," she said very quietly. "You lost your father and Danny and in a way, Amanda. Your family is broken. Only Silver is left, and if you let yourself be her father and someone claims her, or worse, she finds out about her history and leaves, you're afraid of what will happen to you."

Wade kept mute, but his pained dark gaze never left hers.

"The thing is, Wade," Connie said, touching his arm as she spoke the hurtful words, "no matter whether you let yourself love her or not, Silver *will* leave you one day. Nobody stays forever. The only constant any of us have in our lives is God."

"And how do you propose I deal with that?" he demanded, his tone stinging her heart with its oozing pain.

"You enjoy today. Yesterday is gone. Tomorrow is an unknown. All you can guarantee with Silver is right now," she insisted softly. "God is here with you, waiting for you to embrace her and enjoy each second of the life He gives you together."

"You make it sound so easy," he raged.

Connie shook her head.

"It's not easy. It's terribly hard to live in the moment." She swallowed. "Harder still to do the right thing even though you know it will break your heart," she whispered, thinking of her father and whatever had prompted him to abandon her.

"So now you're saying I should find her family?"

"You are Silver's family," Connie insisted. "And no matter what happens, that will never change. Unless you change it."

Wade pursed his lips.

"But if it will ease your mind, or if you feel it

will enrich her life to know others she's related to, why not seek them out? Not now because you need time to build a relationship with her yourself. But someday you could ask them to be part of her world on your terms," Connie coaxed. "Not because you want to give her up, but because you want to make her life fuller, because you want to give your daughter every opportunity."

He still said nothing, but his eyes had darkened to almost black.

"Including the choice of whether or not to leave you," she whispered.

He reared back, rage boiling in his eyes.

Connie longed to reach out and rub away the deep grooves beside his eyes, to put her hands on his shoulders and massage away the fear so he could see the truth.

"Someone who truly loves another wants whatever is best for the other, no matter what the cost to them. That's the very definition of love."

Some inner prompting told her to stop there, to let Wade think in peace. So Connie walked away from him, gathered Silver in her arms and carried the sleeping girl upstairs.

Back in her own room, she sat on her window seat and noticed that Wade had left the backyard. To think about what she'd said?

Connie squeezed her eyes closed. In her mind, she replayed the message with which that voice on the telephone had blown up her hopes and dreams.

If I remember correctly, your father had cancer. He received treatment but it returned and progressed so far his legs were amputated. I doubt he survived.

Eleven years Connie had spent searching for this man, hoping to hear the exact same words Silver yearned to hear. "I love you, daughter of mine."

Wade wouldn't say it, and now it seemed as if her father couldn't.

Casting all your cares on Him, because He cares for you.

"I'm really good at giving advice, Lord," Connie whispered as tears stung her eyes and spilled down her cheeks. "But I'm not very good at taking it. Please help me."

Chapter Seven

"Amanda, can we please cease and desist from these constant wars?" On this Sunday morning, Wade dragged a hand through his hair, wearied by her harping.

"Constant?" she fumed.

"It seems like it. I'm not trying to be nasty, but you're wearing me down. Every day you have some new demand."

"I don't think my expectation of functioning accommodation is a demand," Amanda said in a huffy tone, her eyes spewing her disgust at him.

"I didn't mean that," he said quietly. "Of course I'll have the plumbing in your bathroom checked. But the way you ask—" He saw her stiffen as if preparing for battle and sighed. "Never mind. I'll have the plumber come tomorrow morning, I promise. And I'll ask Cora to cut down on the salt in your food. Anything else?"

"Plenty. But those two are the most trouble-some." She tugged at the hem of her suit jacket then threw her shoulders back. "Also, I would like to know your plans for Christmas."

"My plans?" He sensed something big was about to break. "What do you mean?"

"You must be planning something with all that's been going on around here."

"Nothing unusual that I know of." Where was this leading?

"Then—?"

Following the wave of her hand, Wade glanced around the room. It brimmed with festive decor. Lopsided angels balanced on coffee tables. Strings of popcorn and paper chains of colored paper dipped and bowed across walls and windows.

"I would prefer it if you would instruct that nanny of yours to stop polluting this house with her inferior decorations." Amanda's scathing gaze rested on a particularly unround wreath propped against a wall.

"Uh," Wade gulped. He could imagine telling Connie to stop planning Christmas about as well as he could imagine Amanda enjoying the festive season.

"You can hardly find even a doorknob that isn't adorned." Amanda's exasperation grew. "It's not as if they're well-done decorations either. They're handmade." She spat out the words as if they carried a bad odor.

"By Silver," he said. "Who is only four."

"Almost five. She'll soon be going off to school. She should know what's proper for an Abbot."

"Proper? I did the same thing when I was her age," he said with a smile.

"And look how you turned out." Amanda sniffed in disgust. "I do hope you're not planning some maudlin singsong around the fireplace on Christmas Eve."

"No, I'm not planning that." But Connie might be.

All at once, her eyes widened. "You're not going to put up a tree, are you?"

"Why not?" he asked stupidly, then wished he hadn't.

"Because they make a mess, drop sap onto the floors and smell up the house. It's all silly and sentimental nonsense anyway." Her voice had grown progressively more harsh.

"Amanda." The time had come to stand his ground. Wade tried reasoning with her. "I know it's a difficult time for you, and I empathize, truly. But Silver is a child. Every child looks forward to Christmas. Danny did," he said quietly.

"Don't you dare speak his name!" Amanda's beautiful face hardened. "Not when you're the reason he isn't here." With a shudder, her harsh mask dissolved, and a grieving mother slipped into its place.

Wade wanted to comfort her, but when she stormed out of the room he let her go, staring into the empty fireplace and wondering if he should plan on celebrating Christmas somewhere else.

"Am I interrupting?" Connie hesitated in the doorway.

"It's fine." Wade sank on the arm of the nearest sofa.

"Is something wrong?"

"Just that I can't seem to say the right thing where Amanda is concerned." He sighed, then noticed how well dressed she was. "Where are you off to?"

"Silver and I are going to church. I wondered if you'd care to join us?" She waited still as a church mouse while he thought it over.

Her hair, a mass of shining curls this morning, was pushed off her face with a wide red band that perfectly matched the sash of her ivory dress. Connie seldom wore makeup, and today was no exception. But then, she didn't need it because her skin glowed with health.

"Is this the day of her angel thing?" he asked, only then realizing he'd never really nailed down the date.

"No, that's on Christmas Eve." Connie moved into the study.

Wade noticed her slim legs, emphasized by the pretty red sandals she wore.

"But there will be a practice after church today, so I'm taking along a lunch." She smiled. "Would you like to join us?"

Why not? What good would it do to sit here and stew about the information he hadn't yet been able to unearth—information about Bella's male friend, Silver's father?

"I'd like to go," Wade said and felt immediate relief about his decision. "David's been nagging me about how long it's been since I've been to church. I need to get back in the groove."

"Good." Connie smiled, and suddenly Wade's day seemed a whole lot brighter. "Ten minutes?"

"Sure. I'll meet you at the front door," he promised.

She waved a hand at him and left. A few moments later, her voice was followed by Silver's excited squeals echoing down the staircase.

Wade wasn't going to bother Connie about Amanda's concerns regarding decorations. The nanny was already doing everything he'd hoped she would to enrich Silver's life. He'd watched her blossom under Connie's tutelage, shedding the quiet reticent nature he'd noted on his last visit home. Silver was growing more confident in herself and the crookedly cut green trees, wobbling angels and garish garlands that hung throughout the house were helping her express herself. Wade had no intention of stopping that.

He made up his mind. This year, there would be Christmas in this house. A rich experience, as happy as Connie could make it. For Silver.

Amanda would just have to deal with it.

Wade pushed away the whispering inner voice that reminded him that if he found the information he sought, this might be the last Christmas he shared with Silver.

"God's love isn't like ours. He doesn't get angry and give up when we don't respond the way He wants." The minister's words pinged a resonance within Connie's heart. "This first Sunday in Advent, we talk about the hope of God's gift to us, the birth of Christ and its meaning for us."

Connie sneaked a glance at Wade. He seemed focused on the minister.

"The hopes of those who knew what God had planned was reinforced by the prophets. But most folks wouldn't or couldn't understand that God would send his son as a tiny helpless baby. That was not the answer they wanted."

A missing father was not the answer Connie wanted either. But nothing she'd learned so far suggested her father had stayed in the Tucson area after receiving his treatments for the cancer that had racked his body. Yet no one seemed to know his whereabouts. It was unthinkable that he might have passed away. Connie was getting frustrated with her search.

Why, God?

"As the nation of Israel suffered and waited for their Messiah, they must have asked God 'why' many times. And God's answer—wait."

So perhaps that was her answer, too. There seemed little she could do but wait and hope that God would show her another path that would take her to her father. Mariah Martens, her foster mother, had given good advice.

"You won't get anywhere in understanding God, Connie, unless you embrace His promises and continue to believe that one day you will have answers to your years of questions." Mariah's voice softened to that tenderness Connie loved to hear. "You have to believe that God had a reason for letting it all happen, no matter what you learn."

Which meant Connie had to trust that leaving her without a home or a father wasn't just a cruel joke or a twist of fate. Not an easy feat when her search was continually frustrated by dead ends.

She focused back on the sermon and the reminder that God had not sent the promised Messiah until many years had passed after the prophecies. But He had kept His promise.

When the closing notes of a familiar carol faded away, Silver had not yet returned from the children's program. Connie rose, feeling awkward as Wade rose, too. She wasn't sure how he'd been impacted by the sermon and didn't want to spoil it if he needed time to mull things over. Thankfully David and his sister Darla came over to talk.

"Davy's taking me out to lunch," Darla told her, face beaming with happiness. "Do you want to come, Connie?"

"That's very nice of you, Darla," Connie said, squeezing the hand that had grasped hers. She remembered Silver's talk about a skiing accident. Obviously it had left Darla with brain damage. A conversation with Darla was almost like talking to Silver. "We can't today. Silver has a practice for the Christmas Eve service."

"I know. I'm going to sing," Darla said, her grin huge.

"She sings good," Silver said, bells on her belt tinkling as she slipped into place beside Connie. They walked out of the sanctuary.

"She sings *well*," Connie corrected.

They were quickly surrounded by a throng of people who welcomed Wade back to church.

Silver fell into conversation with Darla.

Connie noticed that Wade smiled, shook hands and accepted good wishes but made few comments, his usual reserve firmly in place.

What would Wade Abbot be like without that guard?

None of your business.

Connie blushed at her own thoughts. These little side trips of curiosity about her boss were happening far too often. She was here to work, not to daydream about her employer like the other silly girl he'd hired.

Connie grasped Silver's hand after the three of them waved goodbye to David and his sister. Then she pointed.

"I thought we could sit under that red pistache tree. With the leaves gone, we'll still get some sunshine," she said.

"Okay." Wade fetched their cooler, picnic basket and a thick blanket from the car. "Not a lot of people know its name," he said, leaning back to look into the tree. "You must be studying up."

"Connie knows about hummingbirds," Silver said. "She put up feeders. We fill them lots."

"I hope you don't mind," she said, embarrassed that she hadn't asked permission before hanging the feeders.

"Why would I? Who could dislike a hummingbird?" he wondered.

"I like to learn about the area where I'm living," she said, forcing herself not to look at him as she unpacked their lunch. "Especially hummingbirds in winter. Everything here is so different from up north."

"Including the lack of snow at Christmas, I'm sure." He smiled. "Do you miss it?"

Connie deliberated over her answer while she settled Silver with a sandwich and some juice.

"I talked to my mother last night. They've just received three feet of snow and are in the process of digging out," she said. "Dad got stuck and had to walk home to get the tractor."

"Ugh."

"Snow isn't all bad." She grinned. "We used to have lots of fun when we got snowed in and couldn't go to school. Dad always made those times so great."

Wade ate for a few moments, obviously deep in thought. But his glance kept returning to her.

"Why don't you just go ahead and ask whatever it is that's bothering you?" Connie murmured, struggling to quiet the rapid beat of her heart.

"I don't want to be rude, and it's really none of my business."

"That never stopped *me*." She ignored his gurgle of laughter, wiped Silver's hands and face and handed her a cookie. "Go ahead, ask."

"Does he mind?" Wade waited to ask the question until Silver had risen and wandered over to peer at the broad-billed hummingbird hovering over a nearby bush.

"Dad, you mean?" Connie set down the rest

of her sandwich and studied her boss. "Mind what?"

"That you're here, looking for your birth father." The words spilled out in a rush. Wade looked sheepish.

"Actually, he's the one who encouraged me to come. He said I'd always wonder if I didn't at least try to find out the truth." She smiled, remembering the conversation. "In the eleven years I stayed with my foster parents, he laid down a good foundation of what a father should be. I hope my dad is like that. That's how I remember him anyway."

"And your foster father doesn't care that you still love your birth father?" he probed.

At first Connie couldn't understand why he kept asking. But then she realized that Wade was comparing her situation to his with Silver.

"No. But then my foster father is a very unusual man. He genuinely loves every kid who comes to their home, regardless of how they respond to him." She offered him a cookie before pouring two cups of steaming coffee. "I asked him about that once. He said he knew what it was like to need unconditional love, and he knew what it was to get it. He was once a foster child himself, you see."

"Um." Wade crunched on his cookie, waited for her to continue.

"Dad says love is the one thing that is both the easiest and most difficult to receive." Wade kept looking at her. His pensive stare unnerved her, but she couldn't stop now. "The thing about love is that you determine how it affects you. By accepting it, you become indebted to the one who loves you. By reciprocating, you create a bond between the two of you. By rejecting it, you throw away a chance to grow a relationship that could enrich both of you, and maybe you forfeit future relationships. Whatever your choice, love has consequences."

Wade didn't say anything, but his eyes had narrowed to mere slits.

"At least that's how my birth father sees it." She sipped her coffee and waited.

"Will you still call him Dad—your birth father? When you find him, I mean?" Wade's inscrutable gaze sought and held hers.

"Of course." What was he getting at?

"Even though he dumped you? Even though you already call another man 'Dad'?" A hint of anger underlay his question.

"The two are not mutually exclusive, Wade." She kept her voice soft. "One dad gave me life, nurtured me for eleven years. Another dad saw me through the years that followed. Both of them have a place in my life."

"I don't understand that." He watched Silver spread the crumbs of her cookie for a brilliant red northern cardinal to sample.

"Why?" Connie touched his arm to get his

attention. "Do you think it's wrong to love both of them, to treat them both as fathers?"

"He abandoned you, Connie." The words grated out between his teeth. His lips pinched together, wrinkling his mustache and emphasizing a cleft in his chin. "Anything could have happened to you. What kind of a father—" He clamped his lips together, shutting off the words of condemnation.

She'd held in all her questions for too long. Suddenly Wade's comments brought everything to the forefront, and Connie couldn't hold back her frustrations any longer.

"I don't know what kind of father would do that," she spat out angrily. "Do you think I don't want to know, that I don't want to ask him myself? Do you think I'm so stupid, so naive and gullible that I've just accepted what he did?"

In spite of her determination, tears escaped her tightly squeezed lids and trickled down to her chin. She scrubbed them away with her fists.

"I'm sorry. I shouldn't have asked."

"I've thought about little else for eleven long years. That's why I'm trying to find my father." She jerked away from his outstretched hand. "I love him," she whispered fiercely, "but sometimes I think I hate him, too. And I have no right to do that."

"Why not?" Wade demanded, his voice unsympathetic. "After what he did—"

"But that's exactly it," she said. "I don't know exactly what he did. A man I spoke to said my father insisted he'd made arrangements for me. That I wasn't simply abandoned." She cleared her throat, met his skeptical glance. "The man said my father repeated over and over that I would be cared for."

"Sure he said that. After the fact. To ease his guilt."

"No." She peered at him through her lashes. "My father told me something before he kissed me goodbye. He said, 'Wait here. Someone will come for you.' And they did." Connie blinked, remembering the moments after he'd left with a clarity that had previously eluded her. "At the time I thought I waited forever, but I remember a clock on a nearby building chiming 'Joy to The World.' The song wasn't finished when a couple showed up for me, Wade. I couldn't have waited that long."

Connie sat silent and let the movie in her mind play through from the moment her father had kissed her goodbye and set her suitcase at her feet, to the arrival of the couple who'd picked her up.

"I'm sorry—"

"He said people named Tom and Tanya would be there to take me to a safe place," she whispered as the long-hidden memories burst into the clear light of day. "And they were, before the song was finished."

"It could have been a coincidence," Wade said.

"No. I wasn't abandoned. He had everything arranged." The memory still left Connie confused, but somehow the pain of that long ago Christmas morning had diminished.

"Other kids are going into the church now, Connie." Silver pressed on her shoulder, her voice anxious. "Isn't it time for me to practice?"

"I think so." Connie closed off everything but the immediacy of the moment and her job. Later. She'd think about it later. She packed up the lunch and rose, waiting while Wade folded the blanket they'd sat on and picked up the basket. "Oh," she murmured, suddenly aware that if he came inside to wait for them and saw the practice, it would spoil Silver's Christmas Eve debut. "I'm sure you don't want to hang around for this."

"I have an errand to run. I'll be back to pick you up in—" he checked his watch "—forty-five minutes?"

"Better make it an hour," Connie said and smiled. "It's the first practice."

"Okay." He accepted his daughter's hug then watched her race to the main door.

Connie turned toward the church and began walking.

"Connie?"

"Yes." Puzzled by the odd tone of his voice, she paused, twisted her head to study him. Wade was staring at her the way he'd stared at Cora's chocolate cake on his first evening back in Tucson.

"Thank you for sharing your private life with me. I know it wasn't easy." He twiddled his keys in his fingers for a moment, then lifted his head and met her gaze. "I think both of your fathers should be proud to have a daughter like you."

Connie wanted to say thank you, but Wade was gone, his long-legged stride carrying him to his car before she could get the words out. For the next hour, she sat in the pew and pretended to watch Silver while she puzzled over the look on Wade's face as he said those words. Sadness, a kind of yearning? Sympathy? What did it mean?

Certainly not that he cared about the nanny, Connie chided herself. She was old enough to know Silver's Cinderella fairy tale of happily ever after didn't come true.

But no matter how hard Connie tried to force her attention back on the stage, she couldn't quite erase the memory of Wade's dark brown eyes softening while they rested on her.

Chapter Eight

On Monday evening, Wade checked his inbox.

Report on Joseph Eduardo Silva, aka José, adopted son of Emma and Eduardo Silva of Brazil, deceased with Bella Abbot. See below for further info.

A shudder of revulsion had Wade closing the email from his private investigator without looking any further. He didn't want to reread the details of his wife's transgressions or face his own stupidity about it. The shame, the embarrassment, the betrayal—he'd left all that in the past. Or tried to.

But this is for Silver, a small inner voice chided. Wade had to ensure her real family was all right, that she would be fine with them. To let her go without doing that was unthinkable. So he drew in a breath, prayed for strength and clicked on the email tab once more. Better to find out what he had to deal with up front. He read the details once, twice and then a third time before his thinking processes froze. How could he have been so gullible?

"Oh. Excuse me."

His misery almost overwhelming him, Wade blinked and looked up. Connie stood in the doorway, her face a mix of emotions he couldn't decipher.

"Sorry?"

"I didn't realize you were in here. I'll come back." She'd said it hesitantly, as if it was the last thing she wanted to do.

"You need the computer?" he guessed. He roused, clicked Print and waited while the report slid out and then closed his email. "I'm finished."

"I can come back," she repeated.

"No reason. It's all yours." He saw her expression and knew something was going on. Her eyes swirled with all the shades of gray found in a piece of Arizona silver. "Anything new on the father front—that you want to share, I mean?"

He wasn't trying to intrude. The past four days Wade had sensed that something was off-kilter in Connie's world, but it was difficult to tell what. Since he'd started paying attention to the nanny, he'd realized Connie was a private person who generally kept her problems to herself while focusing on helping others. Knowing that honed his desire to learn more about the woman behind the nanny facade.

"I'm sure you have plenty of your own difficulties," she murmured.

"Don't we all? But sometimes it helps to share." He waited, preparing to walk away when the silence stretched on. Suddenly Connie spoke.

"The other day, at Silver's party, I had a phone call from the man I met that day you were at the center." She licked her lips and continued. "He said my father had cancer and that it had cost him both legs."

"I'm very sorry." Wade knew there was more. He could see it in the way Connie held herself—erect, taut, as if she was bracing for what was to come.

"The thing is—this man hinted that my father may have died from his treatment." She said the words slowly, as if she couldn't quite absorb them.

"You didn't believe him?"

"I don't know what to believe." She shook her head like someone in a daze. "Ben, my contact at the center, just phoned. A man my dad helped get his high school diploma heard I was searching for my father. He wants to meet me. Tonight. I was so startled I said I'd go." She swallowed, brushed several straggling curls off her forehead. "I have to let the center know I can't make it."

"Why can't you?" Wade noted the way she fidgeted. Connie was not a fidgeter. Something had her scared. A surge of compassion filled him as uncertainty washed over her face. "What's the problem?"

"Tonight's not my night off."

"Oh, right." He debated the wisdom of telling her to go anyway but held his tongue. He had no idea of her feelings regarding this new information, and he didn't want to rush her, especially if she was going to hear bad news. "Well, the computer's all yours." He rose.

"Thanks." Was that relief, or did she think he didn't care?

As Wade moved from behind the desk, Connie eased past him. He caught a whiff of the tangy orange scent of her shampoo, and in a flash, he was reminded of all the intimate little things he missed by not having someone special in his life. But most of all, Connie's scent highlighted the loss of closeness a husband and wife shared, the oneness that Wade had thought he and Bella shared.

For Wade, that bond had been irrevocably shattered that day in Brazil. Ever since then, he'd felt horribly alone. He'd stayed that way by choice, but tonight he realized that the lonely nature of his life was growing less appealing.

Wade had learned to live without all the feminine niceties because he wasn't going to let himself get hurt like that ever again. But Connie was becoming a friend. And she was nothing like Bella had been. He couldn't imagine Connie even planning such a betrayal. She was open and honest, not at all like that other nanny.

You don't really know Connie, his subconscious reminded.

But I want to.

Danger, screamed his brain. *Refocus.*

Connie Ladden was here for Silver. Period.

Wade shoved the printouts into his briefcase and told himself to grow up. He'd faced Bella's infidelity long ago. And renewed his decision never to let his heart get involved again. There was no reason to falter from that path now just because a beautiful young woman had entered his solitary world. No reason, except that Connie made him think of possibilities, of what could be and not what had been. Connie's generosity and sweetness drew him like her sugar feeders drew the hummingbirds.

Wade knew he should leave, but something kept him standing there, watching the nanny as she sat behind the desk, clicking the mouse. The light had drained out of her beautiful eyes. She looked alone, desolate and lost. Wade felt a strong desire to help her—as she'd helped Silver, Amanda, even him.

"Would you like company tonight?" he asked

on an impulse. "I could go with you to meet this man."

"But it's not my night off." Connie's troubled gaze rested on him.

"Technically you won't be off, if that makes you feel better. You could help me choose a Christmas tree. I've been putting it off." He watched expressions flutter across her face as she debated the pros and cons of his offer. "Surely you want to know what this fellow has to say?"

"Yes." She didn't look sure.

"So we'll choose the tree, arrange for its delivery and stop by the center. I wouldn't mind going back there." Maybe he'd see Klara Kramer, or whatever her married name was, again. Wade had been trying to reach her for days without success.

"Why would you want to go back?" Connie's eyes brimmed with suspicions.

"That boy in the wheelchair—Kris? I think his mother is a draftswoman I once knew. I'd like to offer her a job." It would put Wade on Amanda's bad side again, but that couldn't be helped. Abbot Bridges needed the talents of someone like Klara.

"Really?" Connie blinked. "Well, if you're sure—"

She left it hanging, as if she suspected he'd back out. But Wade wasn't going to, because with the arrival of his email he'd realized something. Maybe he did only have this Christmas with Silver before he'd have to let her go. Maybe God had another family prepared for her and this would be the last holiday they'd spend together.

Why shouldn't Wade make it special for Silver the way Connie said her father had made things special? The way her foster parents had made things special. That couldn't be wrong, could it? Wasn't that something God would want him to do for Silver?

"Are you sure about this, Wade?" Connie frowned.

"Not exactly." He hesitated, then decided to sound out Connie about his plan. "I want to make this Christmas one Silver will remember. I want to have all the trimmings, like my father used to do."

"And that includes a tree," she said quietly, one eyebrow arched quizzically. "Even though you realize it's going to irritate Amanda."

"I'm not doing it to annoy her," Wade explained frankly. "I'm doing it for Silver, but I'm hoping it will also help Amanda."

"How?"

"Ever since Danny and my father died, Amanda shuts down at Christmas. It's not right. My father loved Christmas," Wade said. A host of memories swarmed his brain. "He worked hard to create Christmas memories that were an intricate part of his faith in God. Dad wouldn't want Amanda to miss out on the joy of Christmas, even though he can't be here to share it with her."

"She may not see it that way," Connie cautioned. "Not that she talks to me that much, but I think she's struggling to forgive God."

"Forgive God?"

"It sounds odd, I know, but think of it from her perspective. God took her husband and her son. Why?" Connie's shoulders lifted and her head bobbed, jiggling the riot of curls she'd pinned to the top of her head. "Amanda hasn't found a satisfactory answer to that question, and so she won't let God be a part of her life. She even has trouble forgiving you."

"You sound like you actually understand her," he said, marveling again at Connie's insight into his family's dysfunction.

"Of course I understand what Amanda feels." Connie giggled. "I'm the original control freak. Every i dotted and every t crossed—that's me. I know exactly how hard it is to uncurl your fingers from the controls and let God take over, because that's what I have to do every single day."

"Is that what Amanda has to do?" he asked. Connie's silence made him lift his head and study her face.

"Eventually," she murmured, "it's what we all have to do."

"Well, I don't dare say that to Amanda," Wade muttered. "She'll only get more angry."

"Maybe." Connie studied him thoughtfully.

"What are you thinking?" Judging by the spark in her eyes, Wade wasn't sure he should have asked.

"Amanda said something the other day that I think you should hear." Connie waited for his nod before continuing. "She said, 'Everyone thinks I should be over it. They don't understand that I wake up thinking about them and go to sleep thinking about them. I'll never see them again and nobody understands what I've lost.'"

"Believe me, I understand." Wade glowered. "He was my father. Danny was my brother. I've wished a thousand times that I hadn't gone with them that day or that we'd waited out the storm. I'm sorry I ever got behind the wheel."

"Have you told Amanda that?" Connie asked.

"No." Wade wasn't sure he wanted to share those regrets with anyone. He'd kept them contained a long time.

"Maybe it's something she needs to hear. Maybe if you apologized—" She held up a hand to stop his protest. "I'm not saying you did anything wrong, but maybe if you said you're sorry—the way you've just said it to me, maybe then Amanda wouldn't feel so abandoned. Maybe she'd realize that she's not alone in her loss."

"Maybe." Wade thought about that while Connie typed on the computer. Perhaps if Amanda and he could talk openly about his father and Danny, some of the tension between them would dissolve and Silver would feel a tighter connection with this family.

Then maybe that precious girl wouldn't forget about him completely when she was gone.

Wade began mentally rehearsing ways of opening the line of conversation with Amanda. Eventually he became aware of Connie's stare.

"Sorry. I was thinking."

"I know." She nodded in understanding. "It's going to take a lot of prayer."

"And a lot of tact," he added ruefully. "That's for later. For now, when would you like to go to the center?"

"Cora went home early. She wasn't feeling well, so I told her I'd make dinner." For the first time since he'd met her, Connie looked uncertain. "I haven't started it yet."

"We could go out," Wade offered. "For pizza. I haven't had pizza since I came back. Maybe Amanda would come, too." He paused then decided to tell Connie the truth. It was probably silly, but Wade thought Connie might understand his intentions. "I have been trying to be more considerate with Amanda," he admitted.

"I've noticed. And it's difficult, I know," Connie

said, that blazing smile back in place. "She's—not an easy person."

Wade almost laughed at the understatement of those words. But he didn't. Instead he grinned at the nanny as if they were coconspirators.

"I'll go and ask her," he said.

"You might get Silver to go with you when you do. Despite appearances to the contrary, Amanda has a soft spot for Silver," Connie said with a smile. "Maybe with a child present, she'd find it harder to refuse."

"Harder than to refuse me alone, you mean?"

Connie said nothing—just gave him an outrageous wink.

"I'll do that." Wade remained in place, watching her brisk movements. "I wanted to ask you something else."

"Oh?" She paused, hands still.

"I wondered if you had a suggestion of something Silver wants for Christmas." He flushed, feeling like a fool. "Something she's been really longing for?"

"Why don't you ask her?" Connie suggested quietly.

Wade opened his mouth to object, but a voice intruded— a soft, sad little voice brimming with yearning.

I want my God to help daddy love me.

Silver's voice on that first day at the center.

Wade lifted his head, saw the nanny's face and knew she'd been thinking along the same lines. Though neither Connie nor Silver would ever know just how much he cared for the delightful little girl, perhaps there was a way to show the child love without saying the actual words. Something tangible.

"She wants a dollhouse." Connie spoke into the silence, her voice almost a whisper. "An original one that's hers alone."

"Yes, now I remember her mentioning that. Maybe I could build one?" He began structuring it in his mind. It would be a replica of this house. Maybe he could send it with her when she left. Surely then she wouldn't forget him.

"I think Silver would love a dollhouse her father built." Connie smiled.

Not her father. Not since Wade learned from that emailed report that Bella had met her lover before she'd had Silver.

Wade ignored his heart's pinch of pain and studied Connie.

"You're quite something, Miss Ladden," he said, admiration flooding him. "You've got all of us branching out, learning new ways to deal with each other. I appreciate your help."

"I haven't done anything special." Connie kept her head bent, but her red cheeks told Wade everything he needed to know. "I'm just the nanny."

"Hardly," he said as he walked out of his office to find Silver and speak with Amanda.

He realized how true it was. Connie had become an integral part of all their worlds. For the first time in years, Wade liked coming home, knowing she was there with Silver, ready to fill him in on any details he'd missed in a four-almost-five world. Cora seemed happier than he remembered, too. And Hornby couldn't stop singing the praises of the nanny who'd offered to do the weeding in the lowest beds so Hornby could save his arthritic knees. Apparently even Amanda had been able to let down her barriers and confide in Connie.

In fact, in a few short months, Silver's nanny had become necessary to all of them. Connie wasn't just doing her job. She was enriching their lives.

As he paused in the foyer, Wade recalled his father and the many Christmas surprises he'd announced right in this spot. Why couldn't he do something similar, something extra special for Connie, to thank her for making their worlds better? He was fairly certain he could do it without Connie turning into a simpering replica of that other nanny. It would be strictly a business thank-you. Nothing more.

Wade had no idea what his surprise could be. But maybe tonight he'd pay more attention to Connie's discussions with her father's friends.

His heart considerably lighter, Wade took the

stairs two at a time. But the closer he got to Amanda's suite of rooms where he could hear Silver talking, the slower his steps. He could find a way to help Connie. That would be simple.

Convincing Amanda to rejoin life, on the other hand, was going to require some heavenly assistance.

"Don't you just love pizza, Grandma?" Silver grinned, displaying white teeth in a face plastered with tomato sauce.

"Probably not as much as you," Amanda grumbled, dabbing at the mess with one corner of her napkin.

"I think we'd better head to the ladies' room and clean up before we—go to the center," Connie said. She'd been going to say "pick out a Christmas tree" but Wade's shaking head cut off those words. "Come on, Silver."

"I'll go with you. Just to make sure I don't look like her," Amanda said. She rose and walked beside Connie while Silver skipped ahead. "Wade seems relaxed tonight."

"Does he?" Connie tried to be totally focused on her charge.

"Yes, he does. And I think it has to do with you."

"Me? What do you mean?" Connie helped Silver scrub off most of the mess, pretending she was busier than necessary just to avoid Amanda's scrutiny.

"Did you ask him to invite me along tonight?"

"No! It's none of my business whom he invites to a meal." Connie frowned and twisted to stare at her. "Why would you think that?"

"He's never asked me to do anything like this since…" Her voice dropped away.

"Amanda, this pizza thing was totally Wade's idea," Connie assured her, drying her hands on a towel. "Thank goodness. I was supposed to prepare dinner, because Cora wasn't feeling well. I don't cook well."

"You're kidding? You do everything well," Amanda said.

"Not cooking. It terrifies me."

"You know what, Grandma? Daddy said he used to come here when he was little and that his daddy always ordered olives on his pizza. I hate olives." Silver grabbed her grandmother's hand and tugged Amanda toward the door while dancing a happy little jig and humming "Silent Night," accompanied by her ever-present bells.

Connie held her breath. *Please God, don't let anything spoil it. Let tonight be an evening to remember for all them—the first of many.*

"It was nice. I haven't had pizza since—in a long time," Amanda substituted, with a quick look at Connie.

When the child raced over to her father, Amanda paused, her hand on Connie's arm.

"I don't want Wade to pity me," she said to Connie, sotto voce. "I couldn't stand that."

"Why would he pity you?"

"Because I'm cranky and grumpy and bawling all the time," Amanda sputtered. "Oh, fiddle." She turned and hurried back to the ladies' room while dabbing at her eyes.

"What's wrong?" Wade demanded, rising when Connie reached the table.

"Amanda had something in her eye. She'll be back in a minute." He frowned, his suspicions obvious. Connie ignored that. "Do you think I could have a little more coffee while we wait? It's delicious."

By the time they left the restaurant, it was later than Connie had expected. Privately, she couldn't help worrying whether her father's friend would wait for them. Silver picked up on her anxiety and threaded her small fingers into Connie's as they rode to the center.

"Did you eat too much?" she asked sympathetically.

"No, sweetie. I'm fine," Connie reassured, but Silver seemed to know she was faking.

"Are you sad about your daddy?"

"Not really. Just feeling a little impatient, that's all. Like you get about Christmas." Connie caught

Wade's glance in the rearview mirror, a glance that shared her uncertainty.

"Not much farther," he said.

When Amanda demanded to know about the center, Wade filled her in. Connie couldn't speak around the lump in her throat, so she remained silent and clung to Silver's tiny hand.

The place was crowded when they arrived, but as soon as the director spied them enter, he hurried over.

"Connie, I'm so glad you came. Pete says he's only in town tonight. He's got a new job doing long-haul trucking, but he saw your notice and he's very eager to talk to you."

"The same for me, Ben," she whispered, suddenly afraid of what she'd hear.

"You go ahead," Wade murmured. "We'll wait as long as you want." When it looked as if Amanda would protest, he bent and murmured something in Silver's ear. She grabbed her grandmother's hand and urged her to hurry and meet Kris. "I'll be praying," Wade said for Connie's ears alone.

"Thank you. I appreciate that." She inhaled deeply before facing the director. "I'm ready," she told Ben.

Ten minutes later, she wondered why she'd been so afraid.

"So my dad didn't die from the chemotherapy," she said, heart thrilling at the news.

"It hit him pretty hard, but Max was still kicking when I last saw him. I think it would take a lot more than cancer to get him." Pete shook his head. "Never saw a man more besotted with his daughter. Showed your picture to everyone. Connie this, Connie that." His eyes narrowed. "We kinda hoped you'd come to visit."

"I couldn't. I didn't know where he was." Connie explained how her father had left her.

"Figured it was something like that," Pete mused. "Max never did believe the doctors when they said they got all the cancer. And since they took his second leg a few years after they said it, maybe he knew his body better than they did."

"But if he got through the chemotherapy both times, and was okay, why didn't he come and get me?" She couldn't understand what could have kept her father away.

"Oh, honey, he wasn't okay. Max was a smart man who was used to meeting life head-on. He's the reason I got my GED and was able to get this job." Pete sighed. "But over a period of five years, Max lost two legs, probably his dignity and a lot of other things folks who haven't been through cancer treatment don't understand." Pete related a few of his own issues. "Even if they did get all the cancer, and who is ever sure of that? I figure independence is a mighty big thing to a man. Max lost most of his. I heard later that he was having some struggles adjusting to life in his chair."

"You mean he was depressed?" Pete filled in a lot of blanks for Connie, but he also created many more questions that she needed answered.

"I think so, yeah." He nodded, his face thoughtful. "Also, another friend, Joey, told me he thought Max's cancer came back, but that might have just been Joey talking. I can't say because I lost track of Max and never saw him again. I kept writing to him, but my letters were returned unopened. He never got them."

"So either he didn't come back, he was deliberately avoiding you or he died." Neither of the three was palatable to Connie.

"Guess so." Pete checked his watch. "I gotta get going, but if I hear any more I'll send a message to you here. Don't see many of the guys I spent time with here in those days. If you see Max, tell him to keep checking in here. I'll try and meet up with him next time I'm through. You just never know."

"You never do." Connie shook his hand. "Thank you for telling me about my father, Pete. I appreciate it."

"He was a good guy. Proud as a peacock and tough as nails, but that man was gentle as a butterfly. He loved you a whole lot," Pete said firmly. "Don't ever forget that."

"I won't." She reached out and hugged him, reluctant to let go of this tenuous link to her father. But eventually she had to let go and watch him walk away.

"Bad news?" Wade took the chair next to her.

"Good and bad. Dad lost two legs to cancer and apparently survived the treatment, but Pete thinks maybe the cancer recurred. He thinks Dad was depressed. That's all I know." She looked at him. "That and the fact that my father talked about me a lot."

"Because he loved you."

The confidence in Wade's voice surprised Connie. She frowned at him.

"I can understand what he did without condoning it," he told her.

"Is that because you're going to do the same thing?" Since Silver and Amanda were busy talking to Kris and his mother, Connie faced down Wade.

"I'm not abandoning my daughter," he argued, his voice harsh, eyes dark with suppressed anger. "I'm trying to restore Silver to her rightful family."

Connie couldn't stifle her sniff of disgust at his answer. Wade ignored it and continued.

"But if I was fighting cancer and had lost both my legs, I might decide to leave Silver with folks who could take care of her when I couldn't. I sure wouldn't want her around to watch me."

"Why?" Connie demanded, infuriated by his logic. "Because she might cry? Express emotion? Demand to stay?"

"All of those reasons and more." Wade touched her shoulder with a gentle hand that said he understood her need to lash out. "If it's a battle for his life, Connie. No man wants his sweet little daughter watching him, especially if he thinks he's losing his battle. He wants her to be happy and carefree."

"Carefree?" she scoffed. "Do you actually believe that can happen?" She glared at him, knowing Wade would infer she was talking about him and Silver as well as herself. But at this point, she didn't care. "You think a child can be happy without her father?"

"You were," he said very quietly. "Weren't you?"

"He forced me to make a new life for myself," she said, irritated that Wade would condone her father's actions.

"Exactly." He crossed his arms over his chest.

"And the fact that I loved the life I had with him, or that I would have done anything to be with him—" She paused, frowned. "That doesn't count for anything?"

"I don't believe your father made his decision

without a great deal of thought, if that's what you're asking, Connie." Wade's voice gentled, his eyes almost caressing in their softening. "You are a very special woman. I'm sure he saw that as you were growing up."

"Special is one of those mean-nothing words, Wade." Connie couldn't let it go. "I'm no more 'special' than any other kid who just wants her dad."

"I'm sure your father wouldn't agree." He appeared fully in control, but Connie could tell from the tic at the corner of his mouth that Wade was forcing back strong emotions. "Sometimes as a parent you have to make decisions based on what is best for someone else."

"Is that what you're doing?" she whispered, then wondered how she dared question him.

His mouth tightened. His eyes narrowed to thin slits.

"Do you think I want to give her up?" he rasped. "Do you think it's easy?"

"I can see that it isn't." Connie leaned forward. "Because you love her."

"Sometimes love isn't enough." Wade rose.

"Sometimes," she said, rising to meet his hard stare, "love is all God gives us. We have to depend on Him to work out the rest."

For a moment she thought he wouldn't answer. His gaze moved to Silver. She was laughing with

Kris, whose sullenness had completely evaporated. Then Wade's melting chocolate scrutiny returned to settle on her. Connie felt her whole body react to Wade's intense gaze.

"Where does all this faith of yours come from?" he whispered.

She knew that whatever answers she gave Wade wouldn't satisfy him. Faith was something everyone had to work out on their own terms. She relearned that lesson every time she spoke to someone about her father.

"How can you be so certain of God, Connie?"

"Aren't you?" she murmured.

"No," he said starkly. His chin thrust forward. "I'm not. Even though I've been a Christian for years, I don't have the rock solid confidence you have. I wish I did. How can you just blindly believe?"

Essentially that was the same question Connie had asked her foster mother. The only answer she had was the same one she'd been given.

"It's not blind faith. I have questions as you do. As Silver has about you," she said bluntly. "But so far God has never let me down. I have to trust His promise that He will never leave or forsake me, no matter what happens." She lifted her head, sensing what was coming from the way he stared at her.

"Even if your father doesn't want to see you? Even if he's dead?"

Dead?

Wades's words hit like bird shot in the most tender spot of Connie's heart. Would she still trust God completely if it turned out that her father was gone?

And yet—didn't she have to? Wade was so strong, so competent, so able. But deep down, behind the stringent mask of control he refused to relinquish, he was hurting and afraid to trust.

Connie vacillated. Maybe she should just shut up. But her conscience wouldn't let go. Only this morning she'd read a Bible verse that said faith without works was dead. How could she claim to believe in God and not trust Him to care for her regardless of what she learned about her father?

Connie was at a crossroads. She had to hold firm in her faith if she was going to encourage this hurting man to lay his problems at the feet of the only One who could help.

"Even if he's dead, Wade," she whispered. "I'll trust Him even then."

His nod was the only sign that he'd heard her answer. He motioned toward Amanda and Silver. "Are you ready to leave?"

"Yes." Connie glanced around the room. "I've learned everything I can tonight."

"I'm guessing you're not in the mood to get a tree."

"Would you mind if we did it another night?"

She forced a smile to her lips. "Maybe tomorrow? It's late, and Silver is probably tired and—"

"Connie."

The quiet control in his voice drew her attention. His dark brown eyes transmitted acceptance, understanding and something that made her nerves skitter and her heartrate pick up. She was probably being silly, and yet Connie knew that in that moment, Wade was as aware of the electric connection between them as she was. But he didn't avoid her or make an excuse. Instead he smiled.

"I know hearing what you did has upset you. You need time to think it through. Take all the time you need. I can stay with Silver tomorrow if you want to get away."

"Thank you." Connie blinked, surprised by the words. "But—"

"You're always endlessly giving to everyone else. Maybe it's time you slowed down and refilled your own well." His wry smile held a hint of self-mocking. "Believe me, I know how easy it is to get stretched so thin that you have to force one foot in front of the other. The tree and everything else can wait."

So easy—it would be so easy to give in and cry on Wade's shoulder. But in the end, it would only embarrass him and make him think she was like the other nanny, something Connie could not and would not risk. His faith in people was rocky. She would do nothing to increase his distrust.

"It's very generous of you, Wade, and I appreciate the offer, but I think the best thing for me is to keep busy." Connie picked up her purse and rose. "Would you have time to get the tree tomorrow night?"

"Sure." He walked with her toward the others. "But could you make time to talk to me tomorrow before dinner? I want to discuss something with you."

"Sure." On the ride home, Connie sat in the backseat, cradling Silver's tired head while Amanda questioned Wade about Klara Kramer.

All Connie could think about was what Wade wanted to discuss.

Surely he wouldn't let her go, not now, not before she'd found her father—certainly not before she'd done everything she could to make Wade rethink his decision to send Silver away.

But that wasn't the only reason she didn't want to leave. Her heart pinched as the truth hit Connie. She had feelings for Wade Abbot. She didn't want them, but they were there and were growing.

She was falling for her boss.

Chapter Nine

For the first time since he could remember, Wade spent an entire Tuesday without accomplishing one work-related item.

In the morning, he took his own advice, avoided the office and refilled his own well by sharing a chat with the pastor. Then he spent several hours sitting at a park, reading his Bible and praying for help. By noon, he'd scrounged up enough courage to phone Connie and ask her to pray. Then he phoned Amanda and asked to meet with her when he returned home.

The talk had not begun well, but once he'd reassured her that it was not about business, she'd settled down to listen. Wade did as Connie suggested and apologized with heartfelt sincerity.

"I'm so terribly sorry it happened, Amanda," he told her with sincerity. "If I could, I'd change things. I'd gladly give up my own life to bring them back."

"But you can't," she said bitterly.

"No one can, Amanda. But they are in good hands now." Her head jerked up, and a fierce anger filled her eyes. "That doesn't mean I'm discounting your pain. I'm not. Actually I'm not saying anything but that I'm truly sorry Dad and Danny died."

"Why are you telling me this?" she demanded. "Why now?"

"Because it's time I said it." He noticed the weary lines around her eyes, the shadows tucked in their depths. Her grief had aged her beyond her years. "I owed you an apology." It cost to admit that, but in saying it Wade realized how right Connie had been as he felt a heaviness lift. "I wasn't understanding enough. I should have insisted on staying longer to help you through your grief. I sincerely apologize for my thoughtlessness."

"Thank you." Her shoulders lifted a fraction as she inhaled. "Thank you for saying that."

"Can I say something else?" He held his breath and prayed for help.

"I could stop you?" Strangely, Amanda almost smiled.

"You know how Dad loved Christmas. You know the way his celebrations reached out and included so many people." Wade stopped, waited.

Amanda nodded. Tears welled, but she pushed them back.

"Go on."

"I want to make this Christmas like he would have," he said. "As kind of a tribute to Dad and Danny. I want to fill the place with light and joy, the way they did. I want to get a tree and decorate it. I want to hang stockings on the fireplace. I want to invite the carolers in for hot chocolate and have a singsong around the piano. I want all of it."

"You mean you want it for Silver?" Amanda's voice hardened.

"In a way, yes," Wade admitted. "She never knew Dad, never heard Danny's laugh, never saw the two of them dive into the gifts under the tree or sip that eggnog Dad always made. I wish she had." He stopped, swallowed his memories and regrouped. "But mostly, Amanda, I want it for us, to remind us how fortunate we were to love two such special people. And because I want to carry on the traditions they started."

Amanda said nothing. She simply watched him. Wade couldn't give up. Not yet.

"I want to keep Christmas as they did," he continued. "But not if it's going to hurt you."

"So you want my permission?" Amanda bent her head so he couldn't read her expression.

"Actually, I want more than that. I want your help."

She jerked upward, eyes wide. "My help? What brought this on?"

"Actually Connie did. She's been telling Silver about her memories from her foster home, and they are many." He chuckled. "You've probably heard about them. Connie has this rich legacy filled with joy and laughter, and I realized that Silver doesn't have any memories like that because we never gave her any."

"You were away," Amanda murmured.

"And now I'm back, and I want to change things." Wade refused to be drawn into an argument. "Will you help me?"

"To do what, exactly?"

"Whatever you want. However you want," he said. "But I want you to be part of our celebrations."

Silence yawned between them. Connie had warned him to go slowly, not to expect much, so Wade waited for Amanda to absorb what he had said. She studied him for a long time.

"I could help Cora plan the menus. Your nanny won't want to do that." Amanda chuckled with a secret delight.

"She won't?" Wade didn't get it.

"Connie doesn't like cooking. Didn't she tell you?" Amanda tipped her head to one side. "Apparently that rich legacy of hers didn't include much kitchen work outside of dishwashing and making scrambled eggs. She was terrified the other night when Cora had to go home sick."

"She was?" And here he thought he knew Connie. Wade frowned. "I didn't know."

"I think there's probably a lot you don't know about your nanny," Amanda speculated. She tapped the fingernail against her table. "You might want to find out."

A hint of knowing in Amanda's voice made Wade glance away.

"Your father always had a 'trim the tree' party," she continued, her voice introspective with memories. "I haven't kept up with the old gang, so I don't know who to invite, but you could ask David and Darla."

And just like that, Wade's Christmas plans took off.

After his conference with Amanda, Wade sought out a tree and arranged for delivery that evening. When Silver and Connie returned from preschool, he coerced them into helping him retrieve decorations from the storage room. Silver mistakenly opened a box brimming with pictures, and Connie could hardly coax her away from them for dinner. Later, Amanda joined them and remained to supervise the selections for tree decorations.

"A theme tree? Amanda, you are so clever." Connie grinned as she surveyed the array of balls and glittering ornaments sprawled across the coffee table. A few deft movements and she had quickly packed away the discarded decorations. "I've never done a theme tree before."

"Well, I've never done many things you have either, so I guess we're even." Though she tried, Amanda couldn't quite hide her flush of pleasure.

Wade sat on the sofa, content to watch the two women work together planning. When Silver crawled onto his lap, he told himself to relax and just enjoy her presence without worrying about tomorrow. Connie would say God would take care of that.

"When can we put things on the tree, Daddy?"

"Mmm, tomorrow night, I guess." He smiled at Silver's whoop of joy. "David and Darla are coming to help, too."

"Good." Silver tipped her blond head to one side. She touched his cheek, traced the faint line of his only remaining scar from the accident. "Can I have a Christmas stocking, Daddy?"

"Of course." He should have thought of that already, but Silver had never really noticed much about Christmas before. Or maybe *he* hadn't. "We will all have Christmas stockings. But Christmas stockings are very special, you know. You must choose just the right one because you might have it for a long time. What kind would you like?"

"I don't know." Silver was totally serious. "In

the box downstairs I saw that picture of you with a red stocking."

It hadn't been Wade. It had been Danny. But Silver wouldn't know that.

"Should I have a red stocking?" Silver asked, her face scrunched up in thought.

"Is red your favorite color?" Wade asked her.

"No, that's Connie's." Silver thought about it for a moment then climbed down and walked over to Connie. "What kind of a stocking should I have?"

Connie glanced at him and blushed. Wade wasn't sure what caused it; he only knew the additional color in her cheeks rendered her more beautiful than ever, despite the tinsel hanging from her hair and the garland looped around her arms.

Whoa! Here he was noticing Connie again. That would not do. He reigned in his thoughts.

"I think you should have a silver one," Connie murmured, "with lots of bells."

"Yes!" Silver danced up and down and then raced over to Wade. "Can we go shopping for my stocking tomorrow, Daddy? I don't have school. We could go in the morning."

"Sorry, I have a meeting in the morning." Wade watched the joy leech out of her. "But maybe in the afternoon I could go."

"Uh-uh. Klara's orientation, remember?" Amanda shrugged. "You told me to have her start tomorrow when you asked me to offer her the job. Unless you expect me to do the orientation?"

There was a dare in her tone. For thirty seconds, Wade's brain shot out all the reasons his stepmother should not talk to his newest employee and skew her perspective on the company. Then he shut the negative voices down.

"If you could, that would be great," he said. "Thanks."

Amanda looked at him with an odd, confused look that said she suspected he was up to something. Wade kept his expression neutral.

"Well, okay. But I haven't done it in a while," she warned.

"You'll manage." When Amanda's smile flashed, Wade was irrationally glad he listened to Connie's advice. Irrational because he never took advice from others about his private life.

And yet—so far Connie hadn't steered him wrong.

"I was wondering." Amanda paused.

"Go ahead." Wade played with a bit of tinsel.

"Maybe you'd like to invite Klara and her son tomorrow—to help with the tree, and for dinner, I mean. Cora could make some of her delicious lasagna. Everyone likes that."

"Hey, good idea," Wade agreed. "Connie, could you talk to Cora about that?"

"Of course. I'm sure you'll enjoy yourselves."

She lifted the box of old decorations. "I'm going to take these back to the storeroom."

Meaning she wouldn't be here? What was that about? Wade rose and followed her out of the room.

"I'll take these." He lifted the box out of her arms. "You lead the way." He deliberately waited until they were in the narrow hallway before he asked the question pressing on his mind. "What did you mean we will enjoy ourselves? You'll be there, too."

"I'm afraid I won't. Tomorrow is my night off." Connie opened the door to the storeroom, switched on the light and stepped inside. She pointed to a space on the shelf. "You can put them there."

Connie not there? Somehow it didn't compute.

"Can't you take another night?" he asked.

"No." She didn't bother explaining.

Wade shoved the box onto the shelf and grabbed Connie's arm before she could hurry away. "Why?" he demanded.

"This is a family thing, Wade," she said. "A time for you, Silver, Amanda and your friends to share. I'm not part of the family. I'm just the nanny."

There was no hopeful note in the statements, nothing that would lead him to believe that she wanted to be more or expected him to beg her to stay. Connie was simply stating facts. It wasn't her fault he didn't like the way it sounded.

"For this Christmas you are part of our family," he said quietly. "I would like it if you could be there. It's not an order, and I don't expect you to work. It's just—I'd like to have you be here."

Connie studied him for a long time. Finally she murmured, "I'll have to think about it."

"Good." Wade couldn't move.

The shadows of the storeroom created an aura of intimacy around Connie's still figure. Her clear, oval face stood out against the brilliant turquoise of her sweater, intensifying the rich silver sheen of her irises. Her slim figure was highlighted against the white shelves, strong yet flexible, gentle yet incredibly powerful in her determination to do what was right for his family.

Connie was everything most men would want in their life.

He leaned forward and kissed her, briefly touching his lips against hers. Connie froze but only for an instant. Then her lips responded to his with a sweet moan of pleasure. Wade deepened the kiss, asking more. And she responded, surprising him with the intensity of her reply.

Then, as quickly as it had begun, the kiss was over. Connie stepped away from him, her face white.

"I'm sorry," she whispered. "That should never have happened."

"Perhaps not," he agreed, still stunned by his wildly careening senses.

"We should get back to the others." In a flash, Connie had resumed her familiar air of quiet dignity. But she would not look at him.

"Connie." Wade tucked a mass of curls behind one ear and slid his finger under her chin so he could look into her eyes. "I'm sorry if I offended you."

"It's not that," she murmured. She peeked at him then looked down. "I'm the nanny," she whispered.

"I know that." He had to smile at her intensity.

"You're my boss."

"Uh-huh." He waited.

"It can't happen again." She did look at him then.

Wade translated the expressions fleeting through her eyes. Determination. Wistfulness, maybe. Regret?

"If Silver saw us—" Her face flushed a rosy red. "She'd assume things, begin to daydream, plan. I can't allow that. I can't hurt her." She stepped out of the room and without another word left him standing there.

Wade eventually closed the storeroom door and returned to the others. He refused to dwell on his own response to the nanny, choosing instead to revel in Silver's laughter and Amanda's apparent peace and goodwill, even if it was only temporary. He did look at Connie, but she was ignoring him.

Later, Cora brought cookies and hot chocolate. Hornby came in to sound out Connie on his ideas for exterior decorations. It was all so normal that Wade relaxed.

"What do you want for Christmas, Daddy?" Silver asked.

Like that, Wade's perfect world cracked.

Because what he wanted for Christmas he couldn't have—a daughter who was his in every way. A family to share with. Love?

"Daddy?"

"I don't know." He played along, tweaked her nose. "New socks?"

"Connie said you'd say that," Silver shouted gleefully. She high-fived the nanny.

Wade glanced at Connie. She met his look with that solemn, steady scrutiny.

"Really?" he asked.

"Really." She smiled.

"You mean I'm predictable?"

"Sometimes." She stayed near him when Silver went to examine the crèche scene Amanda was uncovering. Her voice dropped. "About the stocking for Silver?"

"Yes?"

"I could make her one," Connie offered. "I have fabric left from her angel costume."

"You don't have to do that. It's a lot of work," he said softly so as not to interrupt the others.

"Actually, I've already started." She shook her head. "But that doesn't mean you have to use it down here. I was going to hang it in her room."

Because she thought he wouldn't remember that kids liked Christmas stockings? It irked Wade that she thought so little of his fathering ability, and yet, why wouldn't she? He hadn't done much that was fatherly for most of Silver's life.

"Of course it should hang down here." The clock chimed. Silver's bedtime. Wade rose. "Could I talk to you, Connie? Privately, I mean. After you put her to bed?"

"Certainly." She frowned, her uneasiness evident. But she didn't ask questions, didn't hesitate or make a fuss. Instead, after Silver had hugged him tightly and whispered, "I love you, Daddy," Connie quietly shepherded the child upstairs, chatting about the things they had yet to do for the holidays.

Wade was grateful for that. He didn't want to explain his idea to anyone else if Connie thought it was a dumb one. But when he turned, he noticed Amanda sitting in a shadowed corner of the room. Then he saw the tears dribbling down her face.

"What's wrong?" he asked, wishing God had made women simpler to understand.

Amanda didn't say a word, simply held up the bright red stocking with Danny's name etched in glitter along the top. He remembered it had been a project the two of them had shared. They'd made one for him and his dad, also.

Wade knelt in front of her, unsure of how to proceed, yet determined he would not give up on his project to draw Amanda back into life, into Christmas—at least not yet.

"Do you want to hang it up?" he asked gently, aware of the careful way her fingers traced the letters over and over.

"No." She sniffed, swallowed. "It's just—I see something like this and all of a sudden it's back."

"What is?"

"The pain. The loss. And then I see you and Silver and I wonder why my child had to die." Tears flowed freely now. "I feel so empty. What's the point of pretending to carry on, to celebrate Christmas? I've lost everything." With a little cry, she rose and fled up the stairs.

Amanda had made his young life so much better. She'd never tried to take his mother's place. Instead, she'd let him figure out their relationship in his own mind. And she'd always been there. He wanted to help Amanda, but how could he if she wouldn't let go of the past?

Turning the problem over in his mind, Wade walked to the French doors and let himself out into the courtyard. The tranquility there was one of the best things about the house and one of the things he enjoyed most about being back home. He often sat out under the stars. Somehow it made him feel a little nearer to God, a little less alone. Now he prayed for illumination but found no solace.

"You wanted to speak to me?" Connie stood by the hedge, hands knotted in front of her.

Only now did he notice that her jeans were rumpled, her sweater decorated with globs of white. Glue, he thought. Her hair was mussed, as if Silver had run her fingers through the tumble of curls and sent them sprawling every which way. Connie's beauty struck him anew.

Wade motioned to a chaise and waited for her to sit. Connie's hair dipped and curled around her face, accenting the angle of her cheekbones and the width of her mouth, the one he'd kissed not long ago. Wade forced out the images. *Keep it businesslike*. He chose a chaise several feet away from her.

"About Amanda—I appreciate your suggestions, but it doesn't seem to have helped," he said. "I apologized, and for a while I thought she was all right. But Amanda just rushed out of the room in tears. It's obvious she still blames me."

"Be patient," Connie advised. "It will take time for her to let go of the past. She's clung to her grief for a long time. It's become familiar. If we could get her more involved with Silver, perhaps she'd start to see new reasons to get involved in life."

"Sounds good." Why hadn't he thought of that? Despite his best intentions to treat Connie as the nanny, Wade marveled all over again at the wisdom of this woman. "So how do I do that?"

"Well, what are some things Amanda used to enjoy?" Connie sat with her hands folded in her lap and patiently waited.

"Anything she did with Danny," he said immediately. Obviously that wasn't going to work. He dredged up the past and locked in on several memories. "Shopping."

"Ah." Connie leaned back on the chaise, lifted her feet up and stretched them out. She closed her eyes.

Wade watched the expressions chase across her lovely face. A frown, a twitch of her eyelids. Then she sat up.

"I have an idea. Perhaps Amanda should take Silver to buy a new dress for Christmas. Something fancy, a bit over the top," Connie suggested.

Wade made a face. "Do I have to go?"

"I don't see why." She chuckled at his show of relief.

A moment later, Wade joined her laughter, glad they'd shed the awkwardness of that kiss and returned to their give-and-take relationship. He felt lighter. Somehow with Connie, things seemed possible again. Life regained its fun. Why was that?

"I was wondering how we'd ever get Silver to change out of her angel costume after the pageant," Connie mused. "But a pretty dress to wear afterward just might do it. And Amanda has such a sense of style that she'll know exactly how to find one."

Connie never had a bad word to say about anyone. She also never discounted his ideas. Connie was the kind of person who found a way to get something done. Wade greatly admired that trait. Actually he greatly admired a lot about Silver's nanny.

Stop it!

"Silver's had her first few ballet lessons, I think. How's it going?" he asked.

"Oh, Wade, if you could see her." Connie burst into a fit of the giggles that chased away the last hint of reserve he'd sensed when she arrived. "Wait—you can." She pulled out her phone and moved nearer so he could watch the video she'd recorded.

When he adjusted the angle of the phone, his fingers brushed hers. Connie didn't seem to notice, but Wade did. And he thought how nice it was to share something.

Then his brain reminded him not to get too close to the nanny.

"Oh." He closed the phone and handed it to her, keeping his expression bland. "Um—"

"Exactly." Connie laughed and tucked her phone into her pocket. "Let's just say I don't think you have to worry about ballet as a career for her."

"Good." Wade winked. "I can't fathom having to sit through endless ballet recitals for the next twelve years anyway."

She giggled at that. Then her face suddenly sobered, and Wade remembered that he wouldn't have to worry about that. He wasn't going to be with Silver in the future.

"You're still intent on sending her away?" Connie whispered, making no effort to distance herself. Instead she seemed intent on his answer.

"More than ever." Something in her face— disappointment?—was too painful to watch so Wade didn't look at her as he explained. "I received information on who might be her Brazilian family. She has a lot of relatives, mostly children. They're near her age. She'll be happy."

"Uh huh." Connie favored him with a dubious look. "Have you done a blood test?"

"I don't need to."

Connie's glare shafted straight to his heart. "You mean you're afraid to?"

Yes! Wade kept himself from blurting out the confession. Lord knew he hadn't been the brother he should have been with Danny. These past few weeks at home had only confirmed his suspicions that he didn't have what it took to be a parent. Even if he was Silver's. Which he wasn't. Connie—now she knew what parenting was all about.

There went his silly brain again. Wade straightened.

"I didn't ask you out here to talk about this."

"I'm sorry." Connie rose, took one step away as she shook her head. "I apologize. I have no business questioning you or your decisions."

"Then why do you?" he asked, irritated by her simplistic view of life.

"I guess I'm trying to understand why you feel you have to let Silver go." She frowned at him, brushing the curls off her forehead and out of her eyes, as if seeing him more clearly would help her to understand his decision.

"I would not make a good parent," Wade insisted.

"Sorry?" She flinched at his glare. "I mean, you already are one. Have been for quite some time. What's changed?"

"Silver's getting older, for one thing. She needs

a mother figure." As soon as the words emerged, he jerked upright, staring at Connie to see if she thought he was implying anything. Which he wasn't. No way. He didn't need a wife in his life any more than he needed the responsibility of a daughter.

Liar.

"Lots of kids don't have mothers," Connie said. "Or siblings."

"I know. But I want that for her." *I don't want her to depend on me alone, because I know I'll fail her.* "I had a very rich childhood. I'd like Silver to experience the same." Wade shook his head. "Look I don't want to get into this discussion with you again. I am going to do what's right for Silver, and I think she'll appreciate it when she meets her family."

Connie continued to stare at him, her face troubled.

"I wanted to tell you how much I appreciate what you've been doing to make things more Christmassy. I know you've gone far beyond your job description."

Connie shrugged, inclined her head and waited for him to continue.

"I've never done this before, but I thought it might be nice if we—Amanda, you, Silver and me—volunteered together to do something special for someone else. The thing is…" Wade stopped, embarrassed now that he had to put the plan into words.

"It's a good idea," she said, resuming her seat opposite him. "Please go on."

He took a moment to appreciate Connie's willingness. He'd asked a lot of her—more than most nannies would do. He was hoping that she wouldn't refuse him this time.

"I don't know any place like that," he admitted. "I thought maybe you could ask someone at the center, get suggestions about something we could all do together. If you're willing, that is."

"Of course." Connie smiled. "I'll talk to Ben and let you know. It's a great idea. Christmas is always better when you share."

"I hope so." The night's darkness did a lot to enhance his reactions to her. At least that's what Wade blamed his spiraling heart rate on. "Have you learned anything more about your father?"

"No." Her shoulders drooped, her expressive mouth tipped down. "Deadends, that's all I've hit. Lots of dead ends. It's as if he's disappeared."

"I'm sorry." It was inadequate, of course. But that was all Wade could think of to say. He'd hoped there would be some clue he could follow up to help her locate the man, but that seemed less likely now. "Did you ever consider that maybe God doesn't want you to find him?"

Connie had been studying the pool and the

flickering lights that created shadows on the bottom. Now her head jerked up, and she stared at him.

"No," she said clearly. "I don't believe that."

"Because?" He hated causing her pain, but the possibility was there and it would be better for Connie if she accepted that. Maybe then she wouldn't be so badly hurt.

"Because I don't believe God would bring me this far, give me the leads I've had and then leave me to flounder. That isn't the nature of God."

"Are you sure?" The question popped out of him without thinking.

"You're an architect, Wade." Connie waved a hand. "Amanda told me that your father planned this house."

"He did." Where was she going with this?

"And you design bridges." She waited for his nod. "How would you like it if partway through the construction, your workers abandoned the project because they couldn't see how on earth you could possibly create the bridge you'd drawn?"

"It's not the same."

"Yes, it is," she insisted. "God is the great designer. He promises that all things work together for good for those who love Him. That means that whatever happens, whether I find my dad or whether I don't, He will work it out to my benefit.

I trust his plan, Wade. That's called faith. I'm not going to start doubting Him now."

With a murmured good-night, Connie left, her footsteps diminishing until only the gentle lap of the water against the tiles sounded in the night.

Wade lay back and studied the sky.

"What is your plan for me?" he asked silently.

He'd told himself he'd made up his mind about Silver. But the question still lurked in the recesses of his mind, a tiny flicker of—hope? For the first time, he fanned that flame, let it grow. Was it possible he could keep Silver, raise her as his own, pretend that other family didn't exist?

And what about Connie? He couldn't imagine this house without her. But how could she stay? Could he keep pretending that what he felt for her was nothing more than a silly crush that would wither and die in time? Could he dare trust his heart to another again?

All of that and more Wade poured out to his Heavenly Father.

And wondered how he'd survive if God told him no on both counts.

Chapter Ten

"These are your work?"

Connie jumped and whirled around. It was past 1:00 a.m. on Wednesday night. She'd hoped no one else would be around at this hour.

"Yes," she murmured.

Wade examined each of the stockings hanging from the mantel.

"I should have checked with you first," she apologized, eyeing her work critically, especially the mistakes. "I'll take them down."

"Why? They're fantastic!" He fingered the tiny bells that formed the letter *S* on Silver's ballet slipper. Then he studied Amanda's stocking, a white high-heeled boot with glittering black buckles and stylish zippers. He moved to examine the one she'd made for him, a black hiking boot with white laces that spanned an intricately stitched bridge.

Connie grew uncomfortable with his silence. It

had been a mistake to do this. She'd told herself that a thousand times, but once she'd started the projects, she hadn't been able to stop. Clearly she'd made a mistake. She startled when Wade burst into laughter.

"I have just one question."

"Oh?" She glanced at him and felt her worries seep away. He liked them.

"Where's yours?"

"Here." She lifted the old style nanny boot with a drab brown flat sole. She hadn't been able to resist finishing it in red laces.

"Very clever. You know you could make a mint selling these." Wade chuckled when she hung the garden shoe stocking she'd created for Hornby and the chef's hat stocking for Cora. "Whimsical and apropos," he said. "Everyone who sees them is going to want one."

"I'm glad you like them." She squished the plastic bags in which she'd carried them downstairs, suddenly uncomfortable being alone with him.

Wade looked tired, the fan of lines around his eyes deeper than they had been. His dark hair was mussed and a shadow covered his cheeks and chin, but the five o'clock shadow only made him more handsome. Even the old sweater he wore with patches on its elbows and pulled threads sticking out here and there enhanced his good looks. Connie gulped and rushed into speech to cover her rising heartrate and the flush of yearning that made her wish too much.

"I found something we could all help with," she blurted.

Wade lifted one eyebrow.

"The center is doing a Christmas carol festival. They'll start with dinner then some songs and end with a little talk by Ben. We can help by going the day before to prepare the food and the tables. If you're still interested," she added uncertainly.

"When is this?"

"Saturday. We'd need to go tomorrow to help prepare—if you want. It's all volunteer. But obviously the more volunteers the quicker we'll finish."

"Tomorrow. So if we do our tree tonight, that would work. I'll take Friday afternoon off—is the afternoon enough?" he asked.

"I think so. Silver and I could go in the morning and help wrap gifts for the kids. The food preparation is in the afternoon. You could meet us there—with Amanda, if she wants to come." She saw the dubious look flutter across his face.

"I don't know if Amanda would be so good with food prep," he confided.

"But she would be good with table decorations," Connie said. "I was going to ask her to work on some with me tomorrow while Silver's at school."

"I'll say it again. You are a very clever woman." Wade shared a smile with her. "I can't imagine how Amanda could resist. Is that hot chocolate?" he asked, glancing at the mug she'd left on a side-table.

"Yes. There's still some in the carafe. I'll get you a mug."

"Don't bother." He waved a hand. "I'll get one myself. Unless you're going to bed now?"

"I'm afraid I'm too wide awake to sleep," Connie admitted. She sat down, tucked her legs under herself and picked up her cup, ordering her nerves to quiet. This was nothing more than a discussion between boss and employer. It wasn't like Wade was going to kiss her again.

You wish.

That was the thing. She did wish. And she shouldn't.

"I found these, thought you might like to share them," he said, returning with a plate of brownies. He held it out for her to take one then sat down on the other end of the loveseat, not a foot away from Connie.

"Thank you." Connie bit into the brownie and stared into the flickering flames, the few embers of the logs she'd lit earlier dying away. She could think of nothing to break the silence.

Apparently Wade couldn't either. Or perhaps he wasn't as bothered by it as she was. He munched happily, apparently oblivious to her. Connie, however, was not in the least oblivious to him and the effect he had on her senses. She scrounged for a polite way to escape, but before she could voice it, he spoke.

"You've made quite a difference to our lives," he said, turning so he could face her. "But I'm not sure you've gained as much as we have."

"I've loved looking after Silver," she said, surprised by his comment. "And it's been an advantage to be located in Tucson, too."

"To track down your father, you mean?"

"Yes." She paused then decided to be honest. "Though I seem to have hit a dead end." Connie did not want to dump her problems on him. "How is the dollhouse coming?"

"I finished the plans, but I can't seem to find time to build it. I was thinking of asking a friend of mine—actually Hornby's son—to build it for me. Jared and I are chums from long ago, and he has an incredible talent with wood."

"But you can't!" Connie said, aghast. She swallowed, struggling to contain her irritation. "I thought this was supposed to be Silver's gift from you."

"It will be."

"But it won't be personal if you don't make it yourself," she said. "Don't you know how deeply Silver would value something you created with your own hands, something you made just for her?" Connie had vowed she would not get herself involved in Wade's personal life anymore, but this—this was too important. "I'm sure Jared Hornby's work is great, but it wouldn't be the same thing."

"Connie, I haven't got the time." He sighed at her expression. "Building the structure isn't all there is to it. It would have to be finished, and that would take hours, even if I had a clue how to put together colors and fabrics or could make the time to find the furnishings that should go in it."

"I can help," she offered without thinking. "I can do the interior decorating or paint, if you need that done. I might even know where you could order furniture, too." She told him of the woman she'd met at Silver's prechool who'd spoken of refurbishing a dollhouse. "It's her daughter's dollhouse that Silver envies. Apparently it was a hand-me-down from the child's grandmother."

"I see." Wade nodded. "That's a very generous offer you've made."

Only then did Connie realize she'd committed herself to possibly working with him for hours. Together. Without Silver or Amanda to buffer them. Exactly what she had wanted to avoid. But working with him on something for Silver would be bittersweet.

"We don't have a lot of time," he mused, selecting another brownie.

"Two weeks," Connie replied, imagining Silver's face. "Can I see the drawings?"

"Sure." He left for his study and returned with a roll of vellum. He spread it out on the coffee table, then sat on the floor. He patted the space beside him. "Sit here. You'll be able to see the details better."

Heart pounding, Connie sat beside him. When his arm brushed hers, she didn't pull back. And when his face loomed only inches away, she couldn't help but meet his gaze as he told her of all the special details he'd planned.

"It sounds wonderful," she said when he stopped speaking and looked at her for confirmation. "I have plenty of fabric scraps to make drapes and cushions. It won't take any time to sew them."

"But you've already done so much," he said, his voice quiet, his eyes intense as they studied her. "The stockings, the decorations, Silver's party, the work with Amanda. I don't want to take advantage of you. I'll pay you for your help."

"I won't take it," she said promptly. "I want to do it for Silver. Please?"

Wade thought about it but finally nodded.

"You're very generous. Thank you."

"My pleasure." The stiffness she'd felt earlier had now evaporated. Connie felt comfortable sitting there beside him, studying the fire while everyone else slept.

"My father always had a fire going at Christmas. It didn't matter if it was warm outside. He said we had to have the yule log burning." Wade glanced at her. "I don't think I ever appreciated how much he gave me—not in gifts but in history and memories. It seems especially poignant now."

"Why?" she asked quietly, wondering at the pensive tone of his voice. "Because you're going to send Silver away?"

"Yes." He frowned at her then turned away. "I know you think it's wrong, but it's what I have to do, Connie. It's my obligation."

"Without even ensuring that she isn't your biological daughter?" Connie ignored her brain's warning and touched his face, turning it toward her. "What if you're wrong, Wade?" she whispered. "How will you feel ten years down the road if you learn Silver actually is your child?"

"Devastated." He turned his cheek into her palm, closed his eyes and sighed. "It's not that I don't want her, Connie, but I have no right to her. She's not mine." He gulped. "I know that now."

"How?"

"The man Bella was with when she died." Shame and pain filled Wade's face. "I had an investigator do some checking. My wife was cheating on me long before she left me, Connie—long before

Silver's birth even." He glanced at her to see if she understood the implications, then quickly looked away.

To see such a proud man bowed with disgrace, to witness dishonor slump his broad shoulders, that was more than Connie could take. She reached out and gathered him into her arms.

"Oh, Wade."

"I couldn't believe it at first—didn't want to, I suppose." He made no effort to move away. "But then I looked back over our marriage and had to admit to myself that it was not the idyll life I'd convinced myself of. After the first few months, we began to grow apart. I knew something was wrong. I just didn't want to admit it—to myself or anyone else."

"Is that why you stayed in South America?"

"Maybe. I might have been able to arrange for someone else to take over earlier," he admitted finally.

"But Silver was a reminder of everything that hadn't gone right." Connie pressed him back so she could see his eyes. "It's in the past, Wade. It's over. And even if that man was Silver's father, he's dead. She doesn't recognize anyone but you as her daddy."

"Maybe not now. But turn your question around, Connie. How will she feel in ten years when she learns we're not related?"

"She'll feel loved, cared for, protected and desperately proud of her daddy," she whispered.

Wade tried to smile, but fear wouldn't let him.

"I'm not saying that you never tell her," Connie said softly. "That's a decision you'll have to make. But how can you make any decision when you don't know the truth?" She held a finger across his lips. "You think you know, but can you really disrupt Silver's entire life—not to mention your own—without having all the facts at hand?"

"I'm scared," he admitted. "I'm desperately scared. "What if this is what God wants?"

"To destroy a family?" Connie smiled. She couldn't stop herself from reaching up and brushing back the lock of hair that had fallen forward onto his face. "You think God, your heavenly father, who loved each of us enough to allow His son to die, puts people together only to tear them apart?"

"I don't know anymore."

"But you need to know on both counts. And God has made it possible for you to have a test done and find out the truth." Connie tightened her grip on his hand. "The truth sets us free, Wade. It allows us to make decisions based on knowledge, not on fear. Truth brings wisdom. Truth takes away the power of fear."

"And if she's not mine?" he asked, his voice ragged, his fingers locked around hers.

"Will you love her any less?" Connie whispered.

"No." His eyes widened. "I couldn't love Silver less. She's in my heart. She's always been there, tucked deep inside me from the moment she let out her first cry." He looked stunned. "Even when I thought I couldn't, no, shouldn't love her, I did."

Connie smiled.

"Isn't that what a father does for his daughter?" she whispered.

Wade silently studied her for several moments. Then he leaned forward and kissed her, hard and fast.

"Thank you," he said, his lips a fraction from hers.

"You're welcome." She struggled to smile, to hide the impact of his kiss as she realized she was moving far beyond mere "feelings" for this man.

"I still don't know what I'm going to do," he murmured, smoothing one hand over her hair and toying with one of her curls. "If it turns out—"

"You have to trust God, Wade. That's your job, your part. God will take care of the rest." She suppressed a shiver of delight when he squeezed her shoulder and struggled to speak calmly. "He'll lead you in the right way if you trust Him."

"I'll try."

Wade seemed content to sit there, holding her. But Connie had to move. This situation was too familiar; it brought back too many memories of another man, another time her heart had become involved. And of the way he'd let her down.

Wade was grateful, that was all. He'd needed a sounding board, and she was it. He was concerned about his daughter. But there wasn't anything between them. When his situation with Silver was sorted out, Wade would be embarrassed that he'd kissed the nanny. He certainly wouldn't see a future between them.

And neither could she.

Because Connie wasn't going to be abandoned a third time.

"I'm getting sleepy. I think I need to go to bed." She eased away from him, rose and picked up their dishes. "I'll put these in the kitchen."

"No, I will. You go rest. You've done more than enough for the Abbots today." He lifted the dishes out of her hands and set them down. Then he grasped her shoulders. "I cannot tell you how much I appreciate your help. You are a very special woman, Connie Ladden."

Then he leaned forward and kissed her again, but this time it was a sweet gentle kiss that reached down to the deepest secret part of her heart. It begged her to respond, to let go and enjoy the rush of emotions that threatened to overwhelm her. But deeper still lay the yearning for a man to love her so deeply that she wouldn't be afraid to pour out all the love that had built up inside.

Only—Wade Abbot was not that man.

"Good night." Connie pulled away and hurried from the room before he could respond.

Because to stay was to risk ignoring the warning her brain kept giving and give way to her heart's deepest desire for a man who saw her as only the nanny.

"It's important, David. Connie's had no success at finding her father, beyond what I've told you. I'm beginning to think he doesn't want to be found," Wade told his friend. "I know I could be opening a kettle of worms, but I still want you to find out whatever you can."

"Why don't you do it yourself?" David asked.

"I haven't got the time. I'm building a dollhouse for Silver." He felt a little bit of embarrassment saying that. But thinking about Silver's face on Christmas morning made it all go away. He lowered his voice. "I took DNA samples into the lab that you recommended."

"And?"

"There's an outside chance I'll find out before Christmas."

"And then what?" David asked.

"Then I guess I'll have a decision to make." Wade remembered Connie's advice from last night. In fact, he remembered quite a lot from last night. Most of all, he recalled the way she'd kissed him then rushed away like a frightened bird. "You and Darla are coming tonight to help with the tree, right?"

"We'll be there," David assured him.

After hanging up, Wade called Amanda. She answered her phone laughing.

"Hi," he said, amazed by the lightness of her voice. "How are the table centerpieces coming?"

"Connie is amazing, Wade. Do you know that? You should be paying her double."

"I suppose you said that while she was present." Wade rolled his eyes at her chuckle. "I might have known. Always trying to cause trouble."

Dead silence greeted his words. Wade winced, wished he'd kept silent.

"I wasn't trying to cause trouble, but I do think Connie is a very valuable employee," Amanda said stiffly.

"You're right. And I was just teasing." He prayed he hadn't burnt another bridge with her. "Listen, Amanda, I wondered if you'd have any problem with Abbot Bridges funding part of this dinner Connie wants us to help out with? It's been a while since we've done anything major for the community. Maybe it's time?"

Surprisingly, Amanda agreed.

"I've already told the office to circulate a memo that anyone willing to help out should be here this afternoon or tomorrow. I've also ordered a large tree to be delivered. You'll be getting the bill for it and the decorations," she told him defiantly.

"Good idea. The center should have called you in right from the start," he said. "You were always better at thinking ahead than me."

Silence.

"Thank you, Wade," Amanda said at last. "Your father used to say that, too. Oh, Connie wants to talk to you."

There was muffled conversation before Connie's voice came over the line.

"Wade, would you be able to pick up Silver on your way to the center? The school phoned. Apparently her teacher isn't feeling well, so they're cutting the day short. They'll be finished by lunch. Twenty minutes?" She paused then rushed into speech. "I'd do it, but I promised Ben I'd help him and I don't want—"

"Connie." He cut across her words.

"Yes?" Her shy response bothered him.

Was she still embarrassed about last night?

"I'll take care of her. No problem. Don't worry. We may be a bit late, though," he warned. "I have an errand."

"Oh. Okay. See you later then."

"Uh, Connie?" He waited until he was sure she hadn't hung up. "Is everything okay—with Amanda, I mean?"

"Better than that," she said, happiness lightening

the words. "I have to go now, Wade. I'm supposed to learn something more about my dad this afternoon."

"Okay. Bye." He hung up wondering what she'd learn. He'd hoped to be able to find Connie's dad and reunite the two as her Christmas gift. But if she'd found him early—well, he knew how much it meant for her.

Minutes later, he was in the car, heading for Silver's preschool, excited about his plans. He was beginning to understand his father's excitement at planning surprises.

Silver squealed when she saw him and flung herself into his arms with abandon. For once, Wade hugged her back, relishing the feel of those little arms squeezing his neck until it was hard to breathe.

"My teacher's sick. Did you know that, Daddy?"

"Connie phoned and told me." He buckled her into her carseat and then got behind the wheel. "We're going to meet her and Amanda later, but first, would you like to go Christmas shopping? You haven't got a gift for Grandma yet, have you?"

"No. Only a card. Connie helped me make it." Silver ran through a list of things she thought appropriate for Amanda.

"I'm not sure your grandmother wants a Baby

Goes to Paris, Silver. Did she say she wanted that? Or the monkey game?" He pulled into the mall and parked.

"No," Silver said, jumping free as soon as he'd unbuckled her. "But I like them."

"Well, this is for Grandma, so it should be something she especially likes."

"Okay. I don't have a present for Connie either." Silver tucked her hand in his and skipped along beside him. "Can we eat first? I'm hungry."

"Sure." Wade let her choose hot dogs though he was fairly certain it would not have been Connie's meal of choice. Once he'd cleaned up the relish and ketchup from her face, they were ready.

Shopping was not Wade's favorite activity. However, he soon discovered that Silver was very good at it.

"Not that, Daddy," she said, discarding item after item. "Something special." Almost an hour later, she finally spied her "something special." "That's Connie's present," she declared, pointing.

"That" was a picture of a farm in the summertime, painted by a local artist who had a stall set up in the mall. Rabbits frolicked in the bright green grass while a flock of ducklings paddled on a sparkling blue pond. A little girl with shiny brown pigtails swung blissfully from a huge oak tree that looked as if it had withstood many hardships.

"It's just like the farm where Connie grew up.

She always talks about the ducks she fed and the swing." Silver dragged on his arm. "Can we get it, Daddy?"

"Yes." Wade gladly paid for it, happy when the artist slipped the picture into an already-decorated gift box. Wrapping gifts was not his forte. "I have an idea for your gift for Amanda." He explained it, relieved when Silver seemed delighted with his plan. An hour later, they walked to the car. "Remember, this is our secret. You can't tell Connie or Grandma."

"I won't." Silver sat patiently while he buckled her in. Then she asked, "What are you going to give them for Christmas, Daddy?"

"I'm going to give Amanda a gift certificate to a spa she likes. I don't know about Connie yet." He hurried to change the topic to the center. That kept Silver too busy asking questions to mention Connie's Christmas gift again. Wade could only hope—and pray—that David would find out something about Connie's father before Christmas arrived.

A brightly decorated wreath was the only exterior change to the center. But inside it had been transformed. A huge pine tree sat in one corner filling the space with its fragrance. Sparkling with multicolored lights, it was simply decorated with chains of puffy white popcorn and red berries. Snowflakes hand-cut from white paper fluttered delicately from its heavy boughs. A white sheet formed a tree skirt, already partially covered with gifts in a sparkling array of papers and ribbons.

"Oh, Daddy, look." Silver stood and gazed at the splendor. "I want our tree to look just like that."

"Hi, there." Connie moved from behind a table littered with paper and decorations. "We're a little behind."

"My fault," Amanda said, laughing. "I got carried away." She waved a hand at the mass of table centerpieces lined up at the front. "Good thing you're here, Wade. You can help set up tables."

A few people drifted in to help as the afternoon progressed, but mostly they were alone. Connie never flagged. Wade couldn't help wondering how she kept going. Her energy seemed endless as she moved between the hall and the kitchen, pitching in wherever she was needed. And when Silver tired, she found a place for her to rest quietly. It wasn't until halfway through the afternoon that Wade noticed how Connie froze each time the door opened, how she hungrily searched each face.

Wade kept repeating a prayer that she wouldn't be disappointed by whatever she learned today.

He'd just finished peeling the last potato when he heard Ben, the director of the center, call Connie's name. Hope fluttered through her eyes as she turned to face the director and moved closer to listen.

"This is Harvey Frank. He was in treatment with your father, Connie."

Wade didn't like the expression in Ben's eyes. This was not going to be good news.

"Nice to meet you, Harvey," Connie murmured, shaking the wrinkled hand of the small man. "Do you happen to know where I might find my father?"

"Sorry, miss. He passed on." Harvey shook his head sadly. "One day he was there, in the bed next to me at the hospital, and the next morning when I woke up, he was gone. Real shame, it was. Max was one of the best."

"You're saying my father died?"

"Well, yeah. One day he was there, and the next day he wasn't."

"I see." Connie's face blanched. She sat down on the nearest chair, fingers fluttering nervously against her hair.

Wade immediately went to her and cradled her icy fingers in his own. Connie looked at him gratefully, but her focus returned to Harvey.

"When was this?"

"About three years ago, maybe. They'd found something in his liver, I heard," Harvey said sadly. "He'd done a couple treatments but got awfully sick from them. Max figured he was terminal. I guess he just couldn't hang on any longer—or didn't want to."

"Oh." The stark sorrow in her voice hurt Wade.

"I asked the nurses about his next of kin, but they didn't know." Harvey shrugged. "Never heard another word about him until I came here and saw your sign on the notice board."

Connie sat staring at him, numb, Wade thought. He took over.

"Thank you for making time to come and explain, Harvey. I know Connie appreciates it."

"Oh." Connie blinked back to awareness. "Yes, thank you."

Ben guided Harvey away. Wade hunched down beside Connie.

"Are you all right?" he asked and then realized what a stupid question it was.

"I don't know. It's so strange. I always thought I'd have a chance to talk to my father, even if it was one last time." She blinked, and a tear formed on the end of her lashes before plopping onto her cheek. "I never really believed he'd be gone."

"You've done enough here," Wade said. "Let's go home." He signaled Amanda.

"Don't worry, honey. I'll finish up the details," she said. "Go with Wade and Silver."

"Thank you." Connie rose and glanced around for her jacket. "I just wish I knew where he was buried."

Wade found her bright red coat, helped her into it and did up the buttons while Connie simply stood there, staring at him. Then he roused Silver. He told her what had happened and asked her to be extra gentle with Connie. Silver's eyes watered, but she scrubbed at them then nodded.

The ride home was solemn. Connie broke the silence occasionally with a memory of her father, newly recalled. Wade let her talk, offering only quiet agreement from time to time. When they arrived, he helped Silver out of the car, but Connie didn't move. He opened her door, undid her seat belt and grasped her hand.

"Let's have some tea, Connie. Then you can lie down."

"I'm not tired," she said quietly, eyes wide, brimming with confusion and pain. "It's just—I don't understand, Wade. I was so sure God led me here. How could I be so wrong?"

"You don't have to think about that right now. It's enough to absorb what you've learned." He drew her into the family room, settled Silver beside her and then went to ask Cora for tea.

"It's her dad, isn't it?" Cora asked.

"A man told her he'd died," Wade said. "It's hit her pretty hard. She's going to need some help to get through the next few days."

"It's about time somebody gave back to that girl after all she's done for us," Cora muttered with a dark look at him that suggested she thought Wade should have done better by her.

And he should have. But he'd been too self-involved.

"I have to make a phone call," he said. "Can you stay with her till I get back?"

"Of course. At least Silver will cheer her up," Cora said. "Thank God for that little bundle of blessings. Our lives would be awfully empty without the little one. We all love her a lot."

Me, too, he wanted to say. But worries about that paternity test kept the words stuffed in his throat. So Wade simply nodded and hurried to the study.

"David, I'm sorry to bother you, but I need the name of that investigator you contacted." He explained what had happened. "I want him to find out where the man is buried. Maybe that will help Connie find some closure."

"Maybe." David stopped. "Getting pretty close to the nanny and her problems, aren't you, Wade? You sure you're the same guy who told me to make sure there wouldn't be any entanglements?"

"This is different."

"Because it's Connie?" David chuckled. "Yes, she is very special. Glad you've finally recognized it."

"She's done a lot for Silver, for Amanda. I just want to help, if I can."

"Uh-huh." Scepticism didn't begin to describe

David's mocking tone. "So the tree trimming is off for tonight?"

"No," Wade said after a few minutes thought. "I think carrying on normally might help Connie more."

"And if you can't find her father's grave?"

"I don't know," Wade told him. "But I have to at least try to help her."

"Just don't get too close," David reminded Wade before he hung up.

Good advice.

Unfortunately, Wade thought it came just a little bit too late.

Chapter Eleven

They were all being very careful around her.

And Connie hated that.

She hadn't meant to be here tonight. This should be a family celebration, and she didn't want to intrude. But Wade and Amanda had convinced her she was a vital part of the decorating plan. When Silver added her pleas, Connie gave in, because she didn't want to be alone.

Christmas meant laughter and joy and fun, celebrations for the birth of a blessed child. Not this mournful sadness. Connie rapped her knuckles on the mantel and waited for everyone to look at her.

"I appreciate your sensitivity," she said. "But this is Christmas, and I want to celebrate it. That's what my father would have done, and that's how I want to remember him. So could we please enjoy ourselves?"

Thankfully, everyone accepted her request to rise above the knowledge of her father's death. By the time David and Darla arrived, Silver was dancing and tinkling, Amanda was chiding Wade for his choice in music and Cora had set out a buffet worthy of any tree trimming party. Then Klara and Kris arrived, followed by Hornby's son, Jared, and then the party really took off.

In fact, Connie thought they'd all but forgotten her sad news when she noticed Wade take David and Jared aside. The three spoke rapidly, but it was the occasional glance at her that bothered Connie. It looked like they were discussing her. She decided to face them out.

"Okay, what's going on?" she demanded.

Wade didn't even try to prevaricate.

"Jared is something of an expert at researching genealogy," he said. "David and I thought he might be able to locate the place where your dad was laid to rest."

"But only if you want me to, Connie," Jared quickly added. "If you'd rather handle it yourself then that's fine."

"It's kind of you to offer, Jared." Connie smiled at each of them, overwhelmed by their generosity. "Kind of all three of you. I'd like to find out, yes, but I don't want you to go to any extra trouble."

"It's our pleasure, Connie." David's eyes expressed his sympathy. "Jared and I are godfathers to Silver, and we both appreciate all you've done for her. We've both seen a big change in Silver, due to you. It's a small way for us to pay you back."

"Caring for Silver is my job," she said quietly.

"We all know you've done more than your job." Wade's dark eyes held hers until Connie had to look away.

"Then thank you. I appreciate it," she said—and meant it.

The party picked up after that. Connie's heart wrenched with bittersweet joy as she watched Silver, Amanda and Wade interact as a true family, gathering in their guests and making them part of their celebration. But the more the group enjoyed themselves, the more Connie felt removed from them.

In that moment, she realized it was because she wanted to be more than the nanny. Every night she dreamed of his kiss. Every morning she awoke realizing anew that he still carried a burden from the past. His shadowed eyes when he looked at her and quickly away told her that whatever he'd felt in that swift embrace, he was too afraid to risk loving again.

When Wade lifted Silver to put the star on the top of the tree, Connie suddenly realized that she didn't belong here. Wade's consideration in asking the others to help him find her father's resting place was an act of friendship. But counting on Wade for anything more would be like counting on her father or her former fiancé. Both let her down. Risk that hurt again? No. No matter how much her heart yearned for more from Wade, Connie knew deep in her soul that he simply wasn't able to give it.

She'd done her very best for the Abbot family. Judging by tonight, they were on the right road. They had David and Jared, Cora and Hornby and now Klara and Kris to help them. They would manage. Besides, if Wade did finally have to send Silver away, Connie didn't want to be here to watch. It was time to leave the Abbots.

Christmas—she'd stay until after Christmas. Then she'd give her notice. Until then, she'd enjoy the time she had left here.

"Connie? Aren't you going to check our work?" Amanda frowned at her.

"Of course." Connie rose and admired the tree, determined not to let anyone know her plans. It was going to be a wonderful Christmas for the Abbots. That's what she had to focus on.

"Your party was great, Wade. I've never seen Amanda so animated."

"Yeah." Wade waited. David wouldn't have called just to talk about the party. Something else was going on. "What's up?"

"Connie's father. I don't think he's dead."

"What?" Wade gulped. "But that Harvey fellow

said—" A mental image of Connie's face when she learned the news filled his brain. But what if David was wrong?

"It's too complicated to go into over the phone. Suffice it to say that Jared and I did some digging. There is no record of Max Ladden dying or being buried in this state."

Wade frowned at David's silence. "What aren't you saying?"

"We think he's still alive. The problem is, we can't find him."

Connie would be ecstatic if she heard there was a possibility she could meet her father again.

"We have to find him," Wade said. "I'll pay whatever it takes."

"I wish it was that easy," David said. "I'm faxing over what Jared uncovered. He's been spending a lot of time on this, and everything he's found leads to a dead end. He believes Connie's father left that hospital on the sly and has deliberately chosen to keep his whereabouts a secret."

"Meaning he doesn't want a reunion with his daughter?" Stunned by the implications, Wade blurted out his thoughts. "She'll leave to search for him when she finds out, David. She desperately wants that relationship. But if her father has deliberately avoided Connie—that is what you're implying?"

"Yes. There could be a thousand reasons, but

I do think he's deliberately gone underground because there is some information that Max followed Connie's life, that he contacted the foster agency several times, asked for information and begged them not to tell Connie."

"If she hears that, it's going to kill her spirit. Reuniting with him is what's kept her going. If he avoided her…" Wade's brain whirled with possibilities. "I've got to think about this for a few minutes, David. I'll call you back, okay?"

He hung up, sank into his chair and swirled around to study old Tucson's pretty skyline through his floor to ceiling office windows. But his brain didn't appreciate the colorful adobe-styled buildings or the Christmas decorations festooning doors and windows, emphasizing the season. All he could think about was Connie and the pain that would make her solemn gray eyes darken when she found out her father not only didn't want to see her but deliberately avoided her.

The question was why.

Wade knew Connie well enough to know the pain it would cause her when she learned of her father's decision. If the man truly didn't want a reunion, if he'd avoided Connie because he wanted to be free of her, Connie would be decimated. If she kept looking, the search for her father could well take her beyond Tucson, away from Silver, away from him. Wade knew full well that she wouldn't give up easily because of the way she'd spoken of finding Max. But if she had to face her father's true abandonment alone, without anyone to help her through it—Wade wasn't going to allow that.

"David, me again. I want you to intensify the search for her father. Tell Jared to get whatever help he needs and go wherever it leads."

"Why is this so important to you, Wade?"

Good question. But not something he wanted to discuss, even with his best friend. Not until he'd thought it all the way through. So Wade made the only excuse he could think of.

"I want to find the man and see if he wants to be reunited with Connie for Christmas."

"And if he doesn't?" David's grave tone sent a warning. Wade ignored it.

"Then I'll tell her that." They covered a few other details before Wade hung up. He made an excuse to his secretary and left the office, walking the streets as he thought through his plan.

It would be his Christmas gift to Connie, a reunion between her father and herself. It would also ensure that Connie wouldn't leave them; she wouldn't have to if he found her father for her.

Because the bald truth was that Wade didn't want Connie to leave—ever. He wanted her to stay, help him raise Silver. Connie made his life complete.

Because Wade loved her?

No. He was afraid to love her. He'd been scared of love for so long, scared that if he opened his heart to that wrenching emotion once more, he'd risk the pain and abandonment he'd felt all over again—abandonment every bit as bad as what Connie had experienced. Love had stripped him of everything but especially his pride. Shame had dogged him for so long. Was that why he was so afraid to trust again?

Connie wasn't like Bella; Connie never ran from problems. She worked them through, no matter how difficult. Connie, with her sweet, gentle, loving spirit, would never betray him. That's why he cared about her.

You told yourself that before, and you were wrong.

The old fears multiplied. Wade quelled them by telling himself it was doubtful Connie felt the same about him, especially after she'd trusted two men and both had let her down. Her words—what had she said?

You have to trust, Wade. You have to believe God is going to do his very best for you. And then you have to hang onto your faith as tightly as you can.

Wade sat down on a park bench. Bella's betrayal hadn't only left him afraid to trust his heart. He'd also been afraid to trust God. He'd finally managed to turn over Silver to the Lord he said he believed in. Could he now trust God with Connie?

That was the crux of the matter. Either he trusted God with everything or he didn't trust God at all. It wasn't about parceling out bits of trust here and there. Faith—real faith—meant he trusted God. Period. It was trust now and hang on to that faith, as Connie said, or accept that he didn't have any faith at all.

"I care about her," he prayed silently. "And Silver. I'm scared I'll lose them both." That's when it hit him.

Silver was his right now. If God asked him to give her up, Wade would have do that. But God had never asked that of him yet. Only his own fears had made him consider sending her away. Fear had kept him from showing that beloved child how deep she lay in his heart.

No more.

Wade jumped to his feet. He walked quickly to his car, climbed in and drove home, letting his secretary know he'd be out for the rest of the day. He didn't know yet how or what to do with his growing feelings for Connie. Hopefully he'd have found her father by Christmas Eve and then he'd reassess.

But Wade did know how he was going to let Silver know she was loved, no matter what the blood tests said. And a certain dollhouse, made by his hands, would help him express that love. He'd better get busy.

With the center's dinner over and the Sunday school Christmas pageant only a week away, Connie had her hands full making last-minute alterations to other costumes she'd offered to help sew. But even with all her busyness, she'd had time to notice that Wade spent hours in the small workshop in the backyard. She hadn't gone out to check on his progress, because she was sure that when he needed her help he'd ask. But as days passed and no request came, she grew worried.

Amanda caught her staring out the window late one evening.

"He's been spending a lot of time in there," she mused as she poured herself a cup of tea. "It reminds me of his father when he was building..." The words died away as Amanda turned to leave the room.

"Amanda?" Connie touched her arm. "It's okay to cry. I know you miss them."

"I do." She wept openly now, her face ravaged. "I've tried so hard to be too busy, to keep myself occupied, but it's just pretend. Nothing's helping. I've prayed so hard. I don't understand why God left me all alone with no one to love."

"But He didn't!" Connie urged her to a stool by

the kitchen bar. "Amanda, God has given you an outlet for your love. You have a wonderful granddaughter who desperately needs you in her life."

"For what?" Amanda said bitterly.

"To tell her things no one else can. Silver is full of questions about the past. I don't know what to tell her, but you do."

"I only met Bella twice," Amanda said.

"Then tell her about those meetings. Be the mother figure she craves. Be there to answer all the other questions she's going to have in the coming years." *If Wade doesn't send her away.* "One day, Silver is going to need to talk to someone who will really listen to her and advise her. You could be that person."

"Do you think so?" Amanda frowned. "I wouldn't know what to say."

"What kind of things did you talk to Danny about?"

"Everything." Amanda mustered a smile. "He was a lovable child."

"So is Silver," Connie assured her. "And she loves you very much. She needs to know you love her, too—that you'll be there for her if she ever needs you."

"Maybe…" Amanda dropped into thought.

"There's just one thing." Connie waited until the older woman looked at her. "You can't put down Wade to Silver. It wouldn't be right. She needs both her daddy and her grandmother in her corner. Can you do that?"

"I guess." Amanda sighed. "The truth is, I've always been a little jealous of Wade. I worried his father would love him more than Danny."

"And did he?"

"No." Amanda smiled. "That man had a heart big enough to love anyone who crossed his path. He loved both his sons very much. And he loved me."

"Then tell Silver about that legacy," Connie said softly. "Let her know that she comes from a family that loves. Whatever was between you and Wade is the past. Let it go. He needs it as much as you."

"Do you think so?" Amanda's eyes widened. "We used to be close, but—"

"You need to be again," Connie insisted. "There's a whole future to deal with now, and Silver is going to need both of you."

Amanda studied her and then finally nodded.

"Yes, Silver is what's important. Most of my anger at Wade was because he found a new wife and baby and I had nothing."

"Not nothing," Connie corrected with a smile. "You have a future, a grandchild who is going to need you to lead her and guide her and a stepson who depends on you to help run your husband's company. Certainly not nothing."

Amanda embraced her, the flowery scent of

her perfume enveloping Connie in a wave of sweetness.

"Thank you, dear. You've encouraged me greatly. I feel like you could be my daughter. You've become so special to me."

"If I helped, I'm glad." Connie let her go. As she watched Amanda walk away, her heart whispered a heaven-sent thank you.

"You're a wonder, Connie Ladden."

Wade's voice shocked her. She turned, saw him standing in the back doorway, half-hidden by the shadows. He looked tired but relaxed.

"How do you always know the right thing to say?"

"I don't." Embarrassed that he'd overheard, Connie changed the subject. "How's the dollhouse coming?"

"Not bad." He poured himself a glass of juice from the fridge and drank it in one gulp. "I could use your help, if you've got a moment."

"Sure." Connie waited until he'd put his glass in the dishwasher then followed him to the workshop. When he opened the door, she gasped. "Oh, my."

It was a dollhouse beyond all others. Not a detail had been missed from the elegant front door with glass side panels to tiny windows that opened.

"Do you like it?" he asked softly.

"It would be hard not to." Connie quelled a

shiver at Wade's nearness. He stood so close that she could feel his breath on the back of her neck. "This is amazing."

"Thanks. Do you think you'll still have time to help decorate?" he asked. "I know you've already taken on some extra work for the Christmas pageant."

Connie bent to examine the house, needing to put space between herself and Wade. She was far too aware of him—another reason she needed to leave here. She studied his work carefully, noting the extra touches he'd added that made the house unique.

"You've spent a lot of hours at this," she murmured, brushing her finger against a tiny sink and bathtub. "Where did you find these?"

"I made them out of clay and had a friend fire them." He hunkered down beside her. "Mostly they're for looks. I doubt Silver will ever put water in them."

"But she could. It's truly amazing. The baseboards, the cabinets—you've thought of everything." Connie rose, unable to ignore the building questions in her mind. "But..." She hesitated. It was none of her business, after all.

"But what?" Wade rose, frowned when she remained silent. "What were you going to say, Connie?"

"What about when she leaves?" she asked

softly. "It's a bit unwieldy to transport to South America."

"Silver's not going to South America," he told her. "At least not yet."

"But..." Connie stared at him, afraid to hope.

"She deserves a happy Christmas. When I get the blood test results, then I'll decide what to do. For now, I'm keeping her. If Bella's relatives want to visit her, they can come here." Wade stood straight and tall, his face rigid yet filled with purpose. "I care about her, Connie. I want to show her that."

"Oh, Wade." Connie threw her arms around him and hugged him, her heart singing with praise that finally he'd seen the light. "I'm so glad."

"So am I." His arms moved around her waist, and he held her close, his breath rearranging the curls against her forehead as he stared into her eyes. "You helped me understand that I was trying to do something God hasn't yet asked of me. How can I ever thank you?"

Embarrassed by her unthinking actions, Connie would have moved away. But his hands drew her closer. "You don't have to thank me."

"Yes, I do. Without you—" He shook his head. "I was ready to send her away. I was so confused and mixed up and determined not to get hurt again." He leaned his forehead against hers. "I was so mixed up about what God was asking me to do. How did I get so far off track?"

"We all do sometimes," she whispered, afraid to hope this embrace was anything more than friends celebrating a decision. "But God is patient, and He will teach us the right way to go, if we let Him."

"Yes. I'm learning that." He lifted his hand, pushed the hair off her face so he could look into her eyes. "You taught me, Connie. You also taught me that opening my heart could be freeing instead of imprisoning."

"Your love is what Silver has wanted all along." Connie couldn't, wouldn't let herself hope that Wade was talking about any other kind of love.

"I'm going to have to work up to saying that word," Wade murmured. "But I think I might actually get there." After studying her for several moments, he bent his head and kissed her softly, sweetly—a tender kiss that asked nothing.

And Connie kissed him back. She couldn't help it. She cared so deeply for this man, wanted his happiness more than she wanted her own. She would leave soon, but in the meantime, she would savor this special time with him.

"Oh. Excuse me." Jared stood in the doorway. His eyes flashed with something that he quickly hid.

Connie moved away from Wade, embarrassed, but Wade seemed to feel nothing like that. He grinned at his friend.

"Connie likes the house," he said with a smile just for her.

"I'm glad." Jared grinned at her. "But it needs some furniture and stuff, don't you think?"

"Yes." It was all she could say.

"I built a couple of beds and dressers. I thought I'd try them out. Okay?" He glanced at Wade, who was still staring at Connie and didn't seem to hear the question.

"You made sofas, too? If you had any extra fabric, I could use it for matching drapes," Connie said quickly, trying to cover Wade's unusual silence. Why was he still staring at her?

"Sure." Jared crouched down and placed his pieces in certain rooms. Then he offered Connie a tape measure and wrote down the numbers she gave him. "Wade's making a couple of coffee tables, too."

"Great." Connie had to get out of here. Wade kept staring at her as if he'd just realized he'd kissed the nanny and couldn't quite believe it. "I'll get started on the cushions and things right away," she promised, edging toward the door.

"With some prayer and hard work, we should finish before Christmas," Jared said. But he was frowning at Wade.

"I'll leave you to it then," she said. She picked up the extra fabric and escaped as quickly as she could, hoping it didn't look like she was running away.

In her room, Connie sat far into the night, stitching tiny furnishings to make the dollhouse more homey. Every so often she took one of the tiny silver bells she'd purchased for Silver's stocking and attached it to a pillow on the end of an embroidered *S*. But no matter how hard she concentrated, Connie could not dislodge the memory of that kiss or her heart's deepest yearning for Wade's love.

Silly, really, because that wasn't going to happen. Wade carried too much baggage from his past. In a rush, the old feelings of abandonment and aloneness returned, stronger than Connie had ever before felt them. For a moment, it seemed as if she stood in the parched Sonoran desert, looking through a window at the lush oasis that was the Abbot family home.

If only—

Connie regrouped and resolutely pushed away the self-pity.

Lord, help me to keep my focus on You. Lead me in Your path. And please show me a way to get past the grief of my father's loss. I wanted to talk to him so badly.

God knew her heart. And He would heal it. Just as He would help her deal with this new love that could never be returned.

Chapter Twelve

"We found Max, Wade." David was almost shouting.

He found Connie's father two days before Christmas? That had to be God answering his prayer. Wade's heart brimmed with thanksgiving.

"Where?" Wade gripped the phone so tightly that he heard the plastic protest.

"Down in Tubac. He's in a wheelchair, very thin and frail, living in an old, abandoned trailer and making jewelry to sell." David sounded jubilant. "Jared figures he's in the last stages of cancer. Max wouldn't say much. He did mention Connie, though."

Wade couldn't suppress the hope. Connie longed to see her father so badly.

"He wants to see her?"

"Not exactly." David's voice dropped. "He talked about the past, mentioned that he knew she was in good hands and how he was glad, because he had nothing to offer her. Apparently his treatments have all failed. There's no hope of recovery."

Wade's heart sank at the news. Connie would be decimated. But maybe if he could just get them together one last time it might help her resolve her issues. He had to at least try.

"Thing is, Wade, Jared doesn't think Max is going to change his mind. He was definite that he didn't want to be reunited with Connie, that he wanted to be left alone." David paused. "Jared didn't say he knew Connie, of course. He was trying to play it low key. But he's sure Max won't agree to meet her. So what do we do now?"

It took Wade less than a minute to decide. This was for Connie, who had gone far beyond the call of duty for his family. He'd do whatever it took.

"Get Jared to email me all the details. I'll go down there myself, this afternoon."

"Okay. Wade?" David's voice dropped.

"Yeah?"

"If you want us to go with you, we will," David assured him.

"Thanks, but this is something I need to do myself," he said. "I appreciate your help though. Tell Jared, will you?"

"Sure. We'll be praying."

"Thanks." Once again Wade cancelled his appointments and took the afternoon off. He stopped by the house to change his clothes and print out Jared's email with all the details about Max's home. Connie and Silver were in the backyard, hanging a Christmas piñata.

"It's supposed to be a javelina pig," Connie explained as Silver raced up to him, shoe bells merrily tinkling.

"Connie said me and Darla can break it on Christmas, Daddy," Silver explained.

"That'll be fun." Wade swung her into his arms and held on, praising God for this beloved blessing.

Silver hugged him back then wiggled free. "Did you come to help us?"

"Not right now. I have to run some errands." He glanced at Connie, who averted her gaze. Embarrassed? Ashamed? Or did she just want to avoid him? "Hang up some mistletoe too, will you, Connie? Christmas and mistletoe go hand in hand."

She peeked a quick look at him, blushed a rich, dark red but finally nodded.

"What's mistletoe?" Silver wanted to know.

"You tell her. I have to go." Wade kissed Silver and on impulse leaned over to smack a quick kiss on Connie's cheek. "See you later."

"Later," she murmured, one hand touching the spot where he'd kissed her.

He was nervous and hopeful and scared—and

filled with anticipation. If only Connie felt half of what he felt for her.

God?

Wade left it in his Father's hands, trying to trust while he concentrated on his mission to give Connie the best Christmas present he could think of.

Unfortunately, Max didn't see it that way.

"Look, I told that fellow yesterday, I've gone to a great deal of trouble to make sure my daughter couldn't find me. What right do you have to come here and ruin everything?" The old man's face contorted with pain as he shifted in his chair.

"Ruin?" Wade glared at him. "Connie has been searching for you ever since she left her foster home. She's desperate to see you again, to tell you she loves you."

"And to ask me a bunch of questions." The grizzled head shook from side to side. "I don't want to get into that. I wish you hadn't come here digging up the past. Let it die."

"Let you die, you mean." Wade struggled for a way to reach him. "Do you have any idea how she feels? You left here there. You never told her why or explained that you were sick. You just dumped her."

"I didn't dump her," Max sputtered indignantly. "I arranged it all very carefully, and then I got out of her life. I thought it would be easier for her to bond with a new family."

"Exactly how would that work?" Wade demanded, echoing Connie's words to him. He was angrier than he'd been in a long time. "Was she supposed to just forget you?" he demanded.

"Yes."

Fury gripped Wade at the pain Connie had endured because of his decision. He was about to verbally lambast Max when an inner voice chided him. *Isn't that what you were going to do with Silver?*

Shame suffused him. *Sorry, Lord.*

"Look, you aren't a father," Max said, defeat dragging down his shoulders. "You can't imagine how it would be to have Connie see me like this— useless, dying."

"Actually, I am a father," Wade said, amazed as a rush of pride filled him. "And I was going to do the same thing as you, send my daughter away because I thought she would have a better life with another family. And then I realized that God had given her to me for a reason—because He thought I was the best father she could have."

Max stared at him, his gray eyes, so like Connie's, glimmering with the faintest spark of hope.

"I understand why you did it," Wade said quietly. "I understand your pride. You didn't want her to watch you suffer through treatment, never knowing if you were going to be able to be there for her when it was all finished. You wanted the best for Connie."

"I still do," Max muttered, but sadness was written all over his face.

"And you gave it to her. She had people who truly cared for her, made sure she understood that she was loved."

"Then why does she need to see me?" Max asked.

"Because you're her dad." The truth penetrated Wade's heart even as he said the words. How stupid he'd been not to recognize it long ago. "Connie needs to know that she has a place deep inside your heart that no one else can take—that to you she is always loved."

"I told her all that before I left her," Max murmured. "She has another family now."

Wade's anger drained away. How could he point fingers when he'd been guilty of the same faulty thinking?

"She could have had ten families. That wouldn't alter your place in her life. Connie needs to hear that you will always be her dad, that you will always love her."

Max stared at him for a long while.

"Why does it matter to you?" he finally demanded.

"Because I care about Connie," Wade told him. "Someday you'll have waited too long, and you won't be able to tell her the things she needs to hear. I don't want there to be any regrets for Connie. I want her to know that her father loved her."

I want Silver to know I love her, too.

Max lowered his head to his chest, clearly thinking about his words.

"I suppose you expect me to see her," he said finally. "Did you bring her here?"

"No, I wasn't sure how you'd react."

"Good. Because I don't want her to see me like this. I can't be her father anymore. I can't even look after myself." Max's face hardened into a grim line. "Just leave me alone, will you?"

"I'll go if that's what you want," Wade agreed. "But I need to say something first." He stared at the man and saw himself, except for the grace of God. "You will always be Connie's father, Max. Your illness, time, money, embarrassment, shame—none of it changes that fact. Only God knows how long you have left to be a father."

Max didn't respond.

"You have a chance to make up for all the Christmases you missed. You could come to my place on Christmas morning. Connie would love that. So would I." He held out an envelope. "My address is in here. If you call the number beneath it, someone will come and pick you up and take you to Connie. All you have to do is say the word. You're welcome to stay at my place as long as you want or need. The decision is up to you. But please think about what I've said."

There was nothing more he could say or do, so Wade left. As he drove home, he prayed that God would show Max what He'd shown him—that being a father had little to do with blood and everything to do with love.

Just one more thing Connie had taught him. If only he could give back to her a fraction of what she'd given him.

Christmas Eve morning, Connie woke up with the birds. She dressed quickly then hurried outside to replenish the seed she'd been putting out for the finches. The greedy little yellow birds darted in for a quick bite while she restocked the hummingbird feeders.

She hummed Christmas carols as she worked, bolting in surprise when she turned and found Wade watching her.

"Is the dollhouse finished?" she asked, trying to cover the awkwardness she always felt around him now. Surely he couldn't tell how much she wanted his kisses to be real?

"Come and see." He led the way to his work-room and flung open the door.

Last night when he'd returned home, Connie had handed him a bag with the things she'd made then quickly scurried away lest he think she was waiting to be kissed again. Sometime in the interim, Wade had arranged everything in the dollhouse exactly as she would have done. The final effect was stunning.

"It's perfect," she whispered. "Silver's going to love it."

"I hope so. And if she does, it's due to you, Connie," Wade insisted. "I couldn't have made it look nearly as homey without your help. Thank you."

"You're welcome." She shifted uncomfortably. When his attention stayed on her instead of the dollhouse, she couldn't comprehend the message his eyes were sending. Or was afraid to.

"Any last minute errands to run today?"

"I thought I'd take Silver out for lunch," Connie told him. "She's so excited about tonight that she'll probably want to put on her angel costume as soon as she gets up."

"Can I join you?" Wade asked with a smile. "I'm pretty excited myself."

"Sure." Connie ignored her brain's objections. She was leaving after Christmas. Why not treasure the last few shared moments with him? "Shall we leave about noon? Or would you rather meet us somewhere? I know you have work to do."

"I want to make a couple of calls to South America," he said. "I'm waiting for a letter, but Amanda and I gave everyone else the day off."

"Oh." South America? The hairs on Connie's arms stood up in warning. *Not before Christmas, Lord, please? Let them have one happy Christmas together.*

"What if I met you at Franco's? It has things kids can do while we wait for our meal."

"Okay." Puzzled by the speculative light in his brown eyes, Connie hurried away to prepare for the day. She needed to get an early start, because she did not yet have a suitable gift for Wade.

She had made him a sweater, but now, on second thought, it seemed too personal. Maybe a book would be better—or candy. Cora said he had a sweet tooth.

Round and round she went in her own mind until Connie grew frustrated. The time she'd spent helping him with the dollhouse had brought dreams of being part of his family. That was impossible, because Wade had made it perfectly clear from the day he arrived that he was not interested in a relationship. Despite those kisses, Connie was certain that hadn't changed.

Maybe he'd been lonely when he kissed her. Maybe he'd needed someone to be a friend. Whatever his reasons, Connie could not delude herself that there was anything more to his embrace, no matter how much she wanted it. Allowing herself to trust a man with her emotions would only make her vulnerable again.

And she'd learned that lesson. Twice.

So this Christmas Connie wouldn't get either of her wishes—not a reunion with her father nor reciprocation of the love that had begun to blossom inside for Wade.

That hurt, but Connie stuffed down her feelings and concentrated on Silver.

"Do you mind helping me with a bit of last-minute shopping?" she asked.

Silver was delighted, so they trekked through store after store, fighting the crowds while Connie searched fruitlessly for just the right thing. With only minutes to spare until they met Wade, she finally selected both chocolate and a book and then hurried toward Franco's.

"Hi, Daddy." Silver held up her arms to be picked up, and when her father did that, she pressed her lips against his cheek. "We're all finished shopping. Aren't we, Connie?"

"Completely finished," she agreed, dredging up a carefree smile that would stop that penetrating look Wade was giving her.

Lunch was delicious and fun as Wade kept Silver laughing and Connie smiling with his stories about Christmas in South America. In fact, she was so entertained that Connie stared at her watch in amazement.

"We have to get home," she said. "Silver needs a bath and her hair done and—"

"Whoa." Wade held up his hand and grinned. "Go ahead," he said. "I'll take care of the check and see you later."

"You are going to come and see me be an angel, aren't you, Daddy?" Silver's anxious face peered up at him, desperate hope glimmering in her eyes.

"I wouldn't miss it for the world, honey," he said. Then he brushed a kiss against the top of her head and returned the hug she gave him. "Not for anything."

Connie gulped down her emotions. At last, she thought. At last he's allowing himself to express the emotions he feels for this child. He loves her dearly. I know he does. He just needs some time to come to grips with what that means.

She drove home with Silver sitting quietly in her seat—too quietly.

"Is something wrong, honey?"

Silver said nothing for several minutes. Connie glanced in the rearview mirror. Silver's big blue eyes didn't glow with their usual spark. They were passing a park so Connie pulled in, knowing the child needed to say what lay on her heart.

She unbuckled Silver, helped her out of the car

and then led her to a park bench. Silver flopped down, and Connie crouched in front of her.

"Please tell me what's wrong, sweetie? Did you forget a gift for someone?"

"No." Silver studied her for several minutes before she spoke. "Do you think my daddy loves me, Connie?"

If she said yes and the unthinkable happened... Connie stalled.

"Why are you asking?"

"Sometimes I think Daddy loves me very much— like today when he hugged me. He squeezed really tight, and I could hardly breathe," Silver explained. "But sometimes I think Daddy doesn't want me to be there. Sometimes I think he wants me to go away."

"Oh, sweetie." Connie gathered the sweet girl in her arms and soothed her as best she could. "Sometimes adults get busy and they forget that little girls need attention. But that doesn't mean they don't care about them."

Silver thought it through for several minutes, nestled on Connie's lap. Then she looked up, blue eyes shining.

"'Sides, I asked God to help Daddy love me," she said, her faith ringing true. "And God heard me, didn't He, Connie?"

"He sure did, sweetie. He sure did." She hugged

the little girl, relishing the precious moment, knowing they would soon be over when she left.

"Too tight, Connie." Silver wriggled free, skipped a few steps and then returned to grab Connie's hand. "We hafta go home."

"Yes, we do." Connie belted her in and drove home accompanied by Silver's rendition of "Silent Night," the carol the children would perform at the concert.

Back at home, Silver raced upstairs to prepare for the bath Connie insisted she take. Connie paused by the front hall table, her eye on the mail.

Christmas is almost here, Father. Please let there be something about my dad.

She sifted through the letters stacked on a glass plate.

And froze.

Santiago Investigations. Postmark—Rio de Janeiro.

Her fingers flirted with the thick envelope as Connie recalled Wade's comments about a letter. Regarding Silver's parentage? Wade was close, so close to fully accepting Silver as his daughter. Christmas was just hours away, a time when the Abbot family could finally reunite, as a family should.

This letter could ruin everything, make him doubt his right to Silver.

"Anything about your father there?"

At the sound of Wade's voice, Connie slid the envelope inside her jacket. *Just for a few hours, Lord. Just so they can have one happy Christmas together,* she apologized.

"Connie?" His hand touched her shoulder. He pressed, urging her to face him. His brown eyes were soft, filled with compassion. "I'm sorry. I know you were hoping for information," he said quietly. "But you know the mail is always slower at Christmas."

"I guess." Guilt suffused her. Wade was being so nice and she was tricking him. Shame filled her, but she couldn't give him the letter. She loved him and loved Silver, too. She desperately wanted them to be united as a father and child should. "I'd better go. Silver's waiting," she whispered.

"Okay." He touched her arm. "You're always telling me to trust God. Maybe this is one of those times when you have to trust Him, too."

"Yes." She moved toward the stairs.

"Connie?"

"Yes?" She turned, wondering if he'd guessed. She felt her cheeks grow hot.

"Did you get that mistletoe?" he asked, grinning.

"I spoke to Hornby about it. He said mistletoe was his job, and he'd hang it where he thought best." Why was Wade looking at her like that?

"Ah. A secret. That will be fun." He winked at her. "What time do we leave for the concert?"

"It starts at seven o'clock. We should be there half an hour early," she told him.

"Okay. I'll tell Cora we need to eat early." He walked toward the kitchen.

Connie glanced both ways and then raced to the study, wondering where she could hide the letter so that it wouldn't be found until after tomorrow. Wade had files spread across the desk. Would he move them tonight? She hesitated.

"Checking email?" he asked, standing in the doorway.

"I was going to." She pressed her jacket to her side, holding the letter there. "But I think I'll leave it for now. Maybe I'll look later tonight." Silver's lilting tones called her. "I'd better get to work."

"Keep the faith, Connie. Isn't that what you're always telling me?" Wade grinned, and her heart took flight.

"I guess it is." She forced herself to smile back then hurried away.

The letter burned against her side. She slid it into a drawer, but she couldn't stop glancing at it, checking, wondering if anyone would have noticed. Had Hornby brought in the mail? Would he tell Wade that it was missing?

"Connie? Aren't we going to have my bath?" Silver stood in the doorway, frowning at her.

"Of course we are." Connie got busy at her job, but when she changed her own clothes later, she couldn't help checking to see if the incriminating envelope was still there.

Thief, her conscience complained.

"I'm not stealing it," she defended herself. "I'm just hanging on to it until Christmas is over."

The words did nothing to ease her guilt, and she couldn't think of anything to say all through dinner or on the way to the church. Thankfully, Silver chattered excitedly, covering the awkward moments. Wade said little, though he kept looking at her as if he knew something wasn't right.

Silver was unusually calm as Connie helped her into her angel costume. She waited patiently for the gossamer wings to be buttoned on and never complained a bit when Connie fumbled putting on her headdress.

"Do you remember your words?" Connie asked, worried that the little girl was having an attack of nerves.

"Fear not," the little girl began. She continued with confidence until she reached the last line. "Unto you is born this day in the city of David, a Savior which is Christ the Lord," Silver repeated calmly.

"And the song Darla's going to lead you in?"

"I know it, Connie. I practiced a lot, and I prayed a lot." She lifted her chin, blue eyes brilliant.

"I'm going to be the bestest angel. Daddy's going to love me."

He already does, Connie yearned to assure her.

"You are going to do very well, and I am so proud of you." Connie hugged her. "I love you, Silver."

"I love you, too." Silver hugged her then backed away. "You go sit with Daddy, Connie. I'll stay with Darla," she said as the older girl wandered up to them. Silver took her hand. "We're going to be great," she crowed happily.

"I really love my costume, Connie. Thank you." Darla beamed with happiness.

"You're welcome. Are you sure you want me to go?" They agreed she should leave, but Connie hung around until their Sunday school teacher gathered them up with the other kids. Then she hurried back to the audience and slipped into a seat next to Wade, feeling awkward and ill at ease.

Because of that letter.

"Everything okay?" Wade asked.

"I think so. Where's Amanda?"

"Sitting with some old friends," he explained. "She seemed to prefer that."

"Oh." She had no chance to say more as the program began.

The Christmas story unfolded simply but beautifully as the children told of the birth of the Son of God. When it was time for Silver to perform, Connie caught her breath and leaned forward. A moment later, Wade's warm fingers folded around hers.

"She'll be fine," he murmured close to her ear. "Relax."

And Connie tried, but it wasn't easy with him sitting so close to her, bringing thoughts of what she'd dreamed of, knowing it was just a dream.

Then a rear curtain opened, and Silver stood in a pool of light, her face serene, arms outstretched. Reverently she said her lines clearly. Not a sound from the audience interrupted.

Then Darla and a group of angels appeared beside Silver. Darla's pure clear voice echoed unaccompanied around the sanctuary as she sang the first verse of the "Silent Night" solo. The other children joined in. Connie was so proud that tears welled at the solemn simplicity the children had brought to this Christmas Eve.

Moments later it was over. Wade pulled out a big white handkerchief and began dabbing at her cheeks.

"Why are you crying?" he asked, his face blazing his pride. "They were fantastic."

"I know. It was beautiful." Connie resolutely stuffed away the hopes and dreams she'd cherished for this Christmas. Her father was gone. After tomorrow, Wade wouldn't be in her life anymore—nor Silver. She had only a few hours of happiness left, and then she'd have to start over again somewhere else. "I'll go help Silver change. Excuse me."

"Did you like it?" the little girl asked the moment Connie found her.

"I loved it. You were fantastic." Connie hugged her. "And you were awesome, too, Darla."

"I was nervous before, but Davy said to pretend all the people watching were clowns," Darla explained. "When I did that, I wasn't nervous anymore."

"Very good advice." Connie helped Silver change from her costume to the lovely organza confection Amanda and Silver had purchased. "You look beautiful, sweetie," she said. And she meant it.

Wade echoed the sentiment and bent over to enhance his words with a hug.

To Connie's surprise, Amanda invited several people to the house after the program. She decided to return home with one of them, leaving Wade and Connie to escort Silver.

"Did you like it, Daddy?" Silver sat in her car-seat, waiting, eyes wide with anticipation.

"I loved it," he said softly. "I've never seen a more beautiful angel."

Silver's glow reinforced Connie's decision to keep the letter until after Christmas, though her conscience scoffed at this logic. When Wade found out what she'd done, he would be furious, perhaps even ask her to leave. But Connie was prepared for that. If she could assist Wade, Silver and Amanda to find happiness together, she'd gladly sacrifice herself, because she loved them.

"You look tense," Wade murmured for her ears alone as guests began to arrive. "Why? They won't bite." His hand cupped her elbow, introducing her to each visitor as a "friend."

Difficult as it was to maintain a calm front with him so close, whispering funny comments in her ear, Connie forced a smile on her face as she greeted the visitors and kept it there when Wade insisted she accompany him as they milled around the house, wishing each guest a merry Christmas. Because these would be among the last precious moments she'd spend with the family, Connie tucked each one deep into her heart. But her hungry gaze kept following Wade, wishing, wanting more than to be called a friend, as desperate as any child the night before Christmas.

Seeing Silver tire, Connie excused herself and took the little girl up to bed.

"Daddy said I was the most beautifulest angel he had ever seen," Silver yawned, holding her hands above her head so Connie could lift off her dress.

"And he was right. You were fantastic." Connie

supervised her bedtime ritual and then tucked the covers around the tiny form, smiling as Silver wiggled, setting off the bell on her quilt. Her big blue eyes grew serious.

"Do you think that means that Daddy loves me?" she asked with the smallest quiver in her voice.

"I think your daddy loves you very much," Connie said, unable to deny this child the reassurance she so desperately craved.

"Then why doesn't he tell me?" Big tears formed on the long blond lashes. "I prayed like you said I should and asked God to help him," she said, sniffing back her tears. "I tell Daddy I love him lots and lots, but he never tells me."

"Oh, Silver." Connie gathered the small body in her arms and cradled her, rocking gently. "Saying the words isn't the important part. People often say lots of things they don't mean, you know."

"I know. Like Reggie says I'm a baby sometimes." Silver sniffed. "But I don't think he means it 'cause he always sits with me at snack time."

"Exactly." Connie smoothed the silver gilt hair and cupped the chubby cheeks in her palms. "You know, some people have trouble saying the word *love*. They're afraid of it, so they're scared to say it."

"You mean Daddy is afraid?" Silver's blue eyes grew enormous.

"Maybe," Connie murmured, "but that doesn't matter, because he shows you he loves you in other ways. You see, it's what is in your heart that counts, and I think love is in your daddy's heart. I'm sure he loves you very much. Just like God does. And so do I." She hugged the little girl fiercely. "As much as I would love my own little girl, that's how much I love you, sweetie."

"I love you, too, Connie, and I'm not ascared to say it." Silver hugged her back fiercely. But a moment later she yawned.

"Time to sleep. You've had a big day, and tomorrow's Christmas. I don't want you to be tired." Connie waited for her to lie down again and then tucked the covers around her.

"I won't be tired on Christmas," Silver mumbled, but she slurred the last word as her eyelids drooped.

"No, you'll be as bright and shining and sweet as you always are." Connie sat beside her, watching the pure, clear face relax and fall into dreamland where little girls didn't have to wish for their father's love.

Connie prayed with all the fervor she had that Wade would finally yield and tell this darling child she was fixed immovably in his heart, that he would never let her go.

But the still, small voice inside her reminded her that she was not trusting God to work things out. She was again trying to arrange matters her own way by hiding a letter that could change everything.

The question was not about Wade. The question was whether she truly trusted God to work things out no matter what she wanted.

Convicted, Connie returned to the room and retrieved the letter.

Confession time.

Chapter Thirteen

Do you think my daddy loves me? Then why doesn't he tell me?

The words dug a trench miles deep into Wade's heart.

He snuck away from Silver's room, down the stairs and hid out in his study, his mind whirling. Why couldn't he tell her what she needed to hear? What was he waiting for?

Everything became a tangle in his brain, and he couldn't seem to sort it out. Somehow his feelings for Silver were tied up in a knot of confusion. He prayed for clarity. Slowly the pieces began to fall into place.

He'd been waiting, biding his time for the right moment—actually, until he was certain no one could take Silver away. But the DNA results hadn't come, and even if they had, there was no guarantee that would make Silver his daughter. Someone could contest the results, argue that he wasn't fit to be her father.

And then what?

To send her away, let her go without her knowing that he loved her more than he loved his own life? It was unthinkable. Memories, dollhouses—what would they matter if Silver never knew he loved her?

Connie knew that, had known it all along. She'd tried to tell him over and over that what his daughter needed most was love. Dear, sweet Connie who'd steadfastly stuck by Silver, protected and cherished her the way her own father hadn't. Connie, who knew what it was to long for fatherly love, had done everything she could for her charge. But as much as the nanny loved her, Connie couldn't give Silver what she craved. That wasn't the nanny's job; it was his.

Tests—what did they matter? It was the heart that counted. Connie's truth once more.

Wade rose, went to the shed and retrieved the dollhouse. He'd just manhandled it through the door when Connie appeared.

"Would you mind lending me a hand with this?" he asked. "I want it under the tree for Christmas morning. For Silver."

"Sure." She had something in her hand, an envelope. She probably wanted to slip it beneath the tree. But she put it down and helped him. Together they set up the furniture that had toppled in the move and rearranged the dolls in various rooms. Connie disappeared upstairs and returned with miniature Christmas decorations, which she helped him hang throughout the dollhouse.

Wade was more than aware of the many times their hands brushed, their glances met, the way she quickly shifted or turned her head. How could he have ever thought she was like that other nanny? Connie was right and good and more beautiful than ever in the soft glow of the Christmas tree lights. She'd nurtured and protected Silver when he couldn't, and even when he should have and hadn't.

He loved her.

And for once the words didn't scare him.

At last they were finished. There was nothing more to do. Wade rose and held out his hand to help her up. When she would have moved away, he grasped her other hand and drew her close.

Wade bent his head and kissed her. He smiled at her blink of confusion and inclined his head toward the ball of mistletoe hanging above them, attached by a white ribbon to the chandelier.

"Merry Christmas, Connie."

"M-Merry Christmas," she stammered.

"I can't tell you how happy I am you're here, with us. You've done so much for this family, for me." It wasn't what he wanted to say. Wade cleared his throat. *Say it,* his brain screamed. *For once, just say the words.* "I've come to care a great deal for you, Connie." Then he kissed her again, trying to show her without words what lay deep in his heart.

For a moment, Connie stood stiffly unresponsive. But then her arms crept around his neck, and she kissed him back so tenderly that Wade knew he'd been right to say it.

Connie wouldn't betray him.

She was the woman he wanted in his life.

A second after that thought, she wrenched free of him and murmured good night, before fleeing from the room. Wade was going to go after her, but he thought better of it. He'd rushed her, sprung it on her without warning. She needed time.

So did he. He needed to think this through. Connie was the woman he wanted in his life forever. He couldn't imagine coming home and not seeing her standing there, a smile curving her lips. Mealtimes and laughter—that was Connie. Joy in a few hummingbirds, pleasure in creating unique individual things for people she cared about. Protecting and cherishing the ones she loved. That was the real Connie.

She would never betray him.

That kiss under the mistletoe had assured Wade of Connie's place in his heart.

But in spite of all that, a niggling voice of distrust

would not be silenced. By now Connie knew he had money. The party tonight must have shown her he had some prestige in the community. How could he be certain those things wouldn't eventually sway her?

Wade walked to his study and sat down behind the same desk his father had used. There on the shelf lay his father's Bible.

If any lack wisdom let him ask of God.

"I need wisdom, God. I need to know for sure." He opened the book and began to read, and as he did, Wade finally understood. Connie was the reason God brought him home. He thought he had to give up love, but God is a God of love and gives His children the very best gifts—love that grows and encompasses and includes. To refuse His gift was unthinkable.

Maybe Connie wouldn't accept him. Maybe she didn't feel the same way about him, though remembering her kiss was a pretty good indication otherwise. The thing was, Wade wanted guarantees, and God was saying life had no guarantees—except the guarantee of God's love.

If Wade didn't have faith in this love—if he didn't trust that God would do His very best for him and act on that—he would never know God's plan for his life. God had done his part. He'd brought Silver and Connie into Wade's life. What

Wade did now was up to him, depending on how much he was willing to trust God.

"Okay, Lord. From here on out, I'm trusting you." Wade opened the safe in the study and lifted out the box holding his mother's engagement ring. "Tomorrow morning, I'm going to tell her I love her and ask her to marry me."

"Wade?" Amanda stood in the doorway.

"Can't sleep?" he asked, sliding the ring into his desk.

"Not until I say something." She moved into the room, her face troubled. "I need to apologize to you and ask your forgiveness."

"For what?" he asked in surprise.

"For not being the mother you needed. For blaming you." She blinked away the tears that filled her eyes. "I was trying to hurt you to rid myself of the pain I felt, and that was wrong. Connie helped me realize that God can heal hearts if we let him."

"Yes, He can," Wade said quietly.

"I'm sorry I wasn't there after Bella died. I don't know the whole story, but I know you were hurting, and I added to it." She shook her head. "I blamed you for something that wasn't your fault. I wish I could take that back, but I can't. All I can say is that I'm proud to call you my son, and Silver is the most wonderful granddaughter anyone could have. She brings joy to this house, Wade. So does Connie."

"Yes." Wade walked over and wrapped his arms around Amanda's tiny form. He held her while she wept for a past that still brought sorrow and then helped her focus on a future that could be filled with joy.

"Thank you," Amanda murmured, completely ignoring that fact that her mascara had made black streaks down her cheeks. Her eyes were clear and filled with joy as she let go of him. She glanced at the desk. "What was in the letter?"

"What letter?"

"The one from South America. I happened to see Connie carrying it upstairs. I thought she'd given it to you already." Amanda shrugged. "Maybe she forgot."

"Maybe." But highly doubtful. Connie more than anyone knew how much he wanted to know the truth of Silver's birth.

Wade's niggling doubts were screaming now. *Betrayed! Betrayed!*

"Anyway, Merry Christmas, Wade. I hope you get everything you deserve." Amanda kissed his cheek then hurried away.

Everything he deserved? Wade sank down on his chair and tried to stop thinking, but his brain would not be silenced. Connie had deceived him, kept back a letter she had to know he was waiting for. Why? Because she was trying to inveigle herself into their lives, so they would depend on her, so he would fall for her?

His mind in turmoil, his heart aching from betrayal once again, Wade went out onto the back courtyard to work off his anger by pacing around the garden.

"God?"

The only response was a whisper in his heart. *Trust.* It kept replaying over and over.

But how could he trust again?

Connie walked upstairs, away from Wade, one hand holding the letter, the other pressed to her lips. He'd kissed her, and nothing had ever been so wonderful. She'd felt light as air, until his words had sunken in.

I've come to care a great deal for you.

Great. But caring wasn't love. She would never love anyone as much as she loved Wade. But it was clear that he didn't love her, not as she needed to be loved. That kiss was just part of the magic of Christmas that he'd been caught up in. It had nothing to do with her. Not really.

The same with her father—it was only a fantasy that she'd tried to convince herself would come true. He was gone. The words she longed to hear could never be spoken.

It was over.

Connie wept for everything she'd wanted, for

the love she'd thought Wade might one day feel, for those precious words her father would never speak. She wept until there were no more tears and only one thing left to do. It was time to stop trying to control things, time to let the Abbots figure out their own futures. She didn't know best. God did. It was time to accept His will.

Connie washed her face, picked up the letter and crept downstairs. The house was quiet, only the tree lights glowed, its wondrous spruce scent filling the air. She slipped down the hall to the study, and using the moonlight flooding in, she moved toward the desk. She laid the letter on it, quickly scrawled her resignation on another piece of paper and then turned to leave. Her sleeve brushed a stack of papers off the corner and onto the floor. She bent to pick them up and froze.

"Wade, this is Max Ladden's address. Don't call first" was all she saw.

At first the words wouldn't compute. Call? Her father was alive?

A sledgehammer cracked her heart. Wade knew. He'd known and yet he'd never said a word. Decimated, Connie crumpled in a heap onto the nearest chair. At least she'd thought she could trust Wade. But once again her trust has been misplaced, only this time her trust in God was also rocked to its foundation.

How could He let it happen again?

"I see you finally decided to deliver my mail." Wade stood in the doorway, his face gray, his brown eyes flaring with anger as he glanced from the bulky envelope to her. "Guilty conscience?"

"Yes." Connie rose, defiant, ignoring her burning cheeks. "At least I admit it. How about you?"

"What are you talking about?" He frowned.

"You're a liar, Wade." She waved the piece of paper she'd found. "My father is not dead. You knew that and didn't tell me. How could you do that?"

He had the grace to look ashamed.

"I was going to."

"Sure you were." She couldn't stop staring at him, couldn't suppress the waves of embarrassment, betrayal and humiliation. She'd trusted this man. She'd fallen in love with him. But he was no different than the others who'd betrayed her. How could she have been so stupid?

"Let me explain, Connie."

"Explain what? I told you how much I wanted to be reconciled with him, how desperate I was to find him. You knew how sad I was that I'd never be able to talk to him. And now, to find out he's alive?" She shook her head. "How could you do it?"

"I was going to tell you, Connie." Wade moved forward and stopped directly in front of her. "Right after Christmas." He hunched down so his eyes were level with hers. "I knew that once you learned he was alive that you'd renew your search."

"And?" She wasn't prepared to cut him any slack. This was her father, a man for whom she'd searched for years. To withhold this information— it was cruel. "What right did you have to not tell me, Wade?"

"The right of someone who cares about you," he sputtered, eyes flaring.

Care. There was that word again. But did it mean love? Waves of yearning washed over Connie when Wade grasped her hands in his.

"All I wanted was...I thought maybe if you had a chance to enjoy Christmas with us, it would make up for not having your dad here. I thought, just this once, that we could be your family—Silver, Amanda and me." He paused, swallowed. "You've worked so hard on Christmas, Connie. I wanted you to enjoy the day without anything spoiling it. I figured we could renew your search for your father the next day."

It was so ironic that Connie burst out laughing, only tears accompanied her laughter, streaming down her cheeks.

"What?" Wade was clearly confused by her reaction. "What did I say?"

Connie struggled to stem her emotions so she could explain.

"I kept that letter back because I wanted you

and Silver to have a special Christmas together. I was afraid there'd be something in it that would wreck everything I'd hoped for the two of you," she confessed.

"Why do you care?" he said very softly.

"Because I care about the Abbots," she whispered. "About Amanda and Silver."

"Uh huh." Wade didn't move, but his dark eyes began to glow. "And?"

"And you," she admitted after a breathless pause. "I love you."

"Oh, Connie." Wade tugged her up and into his arms. He kissed her so tenderly that she could do nothing but respond. Obviously satisfied by her response, he finally drew away, though his hands did not let her go. "What a pair of fools we are."

"We are?" she repeated, hardly daring to hope this was happening.

"I love you, Connie Ladden," Wade told her. "I love you more than life. I love having you here. Watching you with Silver and Amanda has been a lesson in love. You crept into my heart so fast that I hardly knew it was happening. And now I don't want to let you go. Ever."

"But—"

"No buts." He pressed a finger against her lips. "I never wanted to love again, Connie. After Bella, I never believed I could trust any woman again. I didn't want to because betrayal hurt so much." His hands moved to her hair, smoothing his fingers over it. "I didn't believe God was on my side or that I could trust Him. But you showed me that being a child of God means more than merely spouting the words. It means that I have to believe and trust that God is working for my happiness even though I don't see it. And I have to have faith in others."

"Oh, Wade. I'm so glad you've found a new relationship with Him. That's the most important thing." Connie stared into his eyes, hungry for more words of love but half-afraid to believe them.

"So do you forgive me for not telling you about your father?" he asked, still so close she could feel his breath on her face.

"If you'll forgive me for withholding that letter," she said. "I was so afraid—"

"No more fears." He pressed a quick kiss on her lips. "We serve a God who chases fears away."

"Yes." Connie sent a prayer for forgiveness heavenward. God hadn't betrayed her. He'd just taught her a lesson in hanging on to her faith, even when things looked bleakest. "About my dad?" she whispered. "Do you think—"

"Connie?"

"Yes?"

"Do you trust me?" Wade's body went still, as if her answer was the most important thing in the world to him.

Connie stared at him as the question hung between them. What was he asking?

"Can you believe that I never meant to hurt you, that I love you more than I've ever loved any woman?" He squeezed her fingers and continued. "Can you believe that I would never intentionally do anything to hurt you, that I would never abandon you as others have? That I will only ever do my very best for you. Can you believe that?"

He sounded so intense. Connie hesitated. But this was no time for doubts. She had to be certain that her love was strong enough to sustain her through whatever came.

"I can't explain now," Wade said softly, "but I need to know you trust me. I promise I'll tell you all tomorrow. But tonight I need to know you trust me with whatever happens."

Whatever happened.

That was the essence of love, wasn't it? To have faith in the other person regardless of circumstances.

And Connie did.

"I can believe that, Wade, because I love you," she told him openly, honestly. "With all my heart. And I trust you."

"Then will you marry me?" he asked, staring into her eyes so intently that Connie felt he could see everything.

Suddenly she was free of the old feelings of

betrayal, free to love with her entire being. The past dimmed in the dawn of the future, with him. A future of love.

"Yes," she whispered. "I'll marry you, Wade."

He kissed her, a kiss brimming with love and tenderness. Then he pressed her head into his shoulder and heaved a sigh of relief.

"Thank you," he whispered.

Connie stood entirely content in his loving embrace, but part of her wondered why he'd asked those questions.

"I have something to show you," Wade said when several moments had passed. He opened his desk drawer and drew out a box. "This was my mother's. I want you to have it, as a promise that I will always be here for you."

He slipped the ring on her finger and sealed their pledge with a kiss. Then they sat in front of the Christmas tree and reminded each other of the many ways God had led them together.

"We need to tuck this moment into our hearts and remember it," Connie whispered as the clock chimed midnight. "If we trust God, He'll always do His best for us."

"Yes. Merry Christmas, darling." Wade kissed her.

Connie smiled.

"Merry Christmas. But what was that for?"

"For love." Wade pointed upward. A cluster of

mistletoe hung directly above them. "Good old Hornby."

"I wonder where else he's hidden them." Connie glanced around.

"You can look tomorrow," Wade said, his mouth quirked in a smug smile. "I'll help you."

"It is tomorrow." Connie kissed his cheek then rose. "Time to fill those stockings. I can hardly wait for morning."

"Me, neither," Wade murmured quizzically. He winked.

Connie went to bed, but she had a hard time falling asleep. Between memories of the day her father had left her and her brimming curiosity about Wade's unusual look, sleep eluded her.

Chapter Fourteen

Connie sat on the side of her bed, staring at the gorgeous diamond ring Wade had slipped onto her finger last night. She'd hardly slept, had been up for ages, but she wasn't tired. She was elated, barely able to believe her dreams had come true.

Well, not all her dreams.

A swift sadness enveloped her, but after a quick prayer she pushed it away. God had blessed her with much. He knew what He was doing. She would leave her father in his hands, too.

The sound of the doorbell echoed up the stairs. Then Silver's quick feet, tapping across the hall and down the steps followed. And yet the doorbell rang again. Then a third time.

Curious, Connie checked her reflection quickly before descending. Why didn't someone answer?

Wade was waiting for her at the bottom of the stairs, his face blazing his love and chasing away any doubts she may have had. He slid his arm around her waist and hugged her.

"Why doesn't someone answer the door?" Amanda asked, emerging from the other end of the hall. "It's been ringing forever."

"Good. We're all here," was all Wade said.

"Now, Daddy?" Silver asked.

"Yes. Right now, sweetheart."

The love in those words, the adoration glowing in his dark eyes—no one could doubt that Wade loved his daughter. Or her. Connie basked in the warm glow of that love.

Silver threw open the door.

"Merry Christmas, darling Connie," Wade murmured, turning her so she faced the door.

A man in a wheelchair sat on the steps. He was stooped and bent, battered by life, more gray than she remembered. But it was her father.

"Dad?" And then she was in his arms, reveling in the reunion she'd sought for so long.

It was Silver who insisted they talk in the family room, Silver who kept hold of Connie's hand as her father explained that he'd left Connie behind to fight a terrible battle with cancer that he was still engaged in and Silver who touched the old man's cheek when his voice faltered.

Then Wade kissed Connie's cheek and whispered, "You two need to talk. We'll give you some privacy."

He took Silver's hand, and together they left the room with Amanda.

Haltingly, without looking at her, Max apologized. He spoke of his shame about his impoverished situation, his feeling that he had nothing to offer Connie, the fear that he would only be an encumbrance or that she would hate him for abandoning her.

"You'd already started treatment when you left me there, hadn't you?" she asked. "I kept thinking about that day last night. You could hardly lift my suitcase, and you were short of breath. And perspiring," she added quietly.

"I'd gone through two sessions by then," Max admitted. "I thought I could go through it without you knowing, but the two times took everything I had. There were four more to go. I knew I couldn't have you there when I couldn't look after you."

"Oh, Dad. I'm so sorry you had to go through that." Connie knelt before him and laid her head on his lap. "At first, yes, I can understand why you needed to do it on your own. I would have been too much trouble. But later?" She lifted her head and peered into his eyes. "Why didn't you come get me later when it was over?"

"Because it was never over." His fingers brushed over her hair. "It won't be over until I die."

The truth was harsh, but the words so precious when her father told her he'd been following her life and had kept track of her until she moved from North Dakota.

"I was going to come and get you after I lost my first leg," he murmured, "but the cancer came back again and again. I know how pitifully disgusting I look. I didn't want you to see me like this. I wanted you to remember me as I was."

"Do you think I care how you look, Dad?" Connie demanded. "I love you."

She was ready to tell him of her sorrow, feelings of abandonment and years of longing to know where he was, when Silver's fingers closed around hers. The little girl smiled. Wade did the same, as if to say, "What does the past matter? You have the present. And the future."

Connie let it go.

"I love you, Dad," she repeated. "I always will." She wrapped her arms around him and hung on despite the reserve that stiffened his body.

After several minutes, Max relaxed and hugged her back. Connie couldn't have asked for any better Christmas gift.

"You have a very persuasive fellow," Max told her. "I had no intention of coming here. In fact, I wouldn't have, but Wade wouldn't give up."

"Yes, that's what I love about him," Connie said sharing a look of love with the man who'd made her Christmas dream come true.

Father and daughter caught up, shared stories

and hugged over and over again until Silver finally demanded, "Aren't we ever going to open our Christmas gifts?"

Everyone burst out laughing.

"Yes, we are," Wade said. He rose and led the little girl to the huge box with her name on it. He knelt down to her level.

"This is my gift to you, Silver. Because you are my little girl, and I love you very much. I always want you to be happy. Merry Christmas." Wade drew her into his arms and held her tight as Silver's big blue eyes filled with tears.

"I love you, too, Daddy," she whispered, clinging to him. "God answered my prayers, too," she said to Connie, her blue eyes huge.

"He certainly did," Connie agreed.

Curiosity soon got the better of the little girl. She jumped out of her father's arms and stood in front of the box.

"It's so big. How do I open it?"

"I'll help. That's what daddies do," Wade said proudly. He beckoned Connie to come help him lift the big box away.

"Oh, Daddy!" Silver danced around the dollhouse, threw herself into his arms then lurched away, too excited to stay still. She bent to peek inside, flattened herself on the floor. "It has dollies and furniture and everything."

"Connie and Uncle David and Uncle Jared

helped with that," Wade said, drawing Connie to him as if he couldn't bear for them to be separated. "And Grandma helped with the roof."

"I tried, in spite of your father's advice," Amanda said in a dry tone with a teasing glance at Wade.

"All of your family worked to make this surprise for you, Silver," Wade said softly. "Because we love you."

Connie's heart squeezed tight at Wade's words. Here was the answer to her prayer for the Abbots—father and daughter together and Amanda joining in.

It was odd, she thought, holding her father's hand as they all watched Silver investigate her dollhouse. She'd once had so many questions for her father. Now that he was here, they didn't matter. He was here, he loved her. That was enough.

"Silver, don't you have some gifts?" Wade prompted after Amanda had brought in a carafe of coffee and some mugs.

"Oh." The little girl cast one last longing look at her dollhouse, then scampered behind the tree to retrieve a package. "This is for you, Grandma." She grinned with delight when Amanda oohed and aahed over the portrait of Silver. "And this is for you, Connie."

Connie accepted the package, expecting a picture of Silver. Instead, she was stunned by the lovely pastoral scene. "This is beautiful," she said, hugging the little girl.

"It's like your farm, isn't it?" Silver asked. "Can we go and visit there, Daddy, after you and Connie get married?"

Connie glanced at Wade. "You told her?"

"He's told everyone." Amanda laughed. "As if we wouldn't have known just by looking at him."

"I couldn't keep it to myself," he said, kissing Connie briefly. He laughed at her startled look and pointed up. "Hornby has them all around the house, so get used to it."

Connie presented her gifts to the others. A paint set for Silver, who'd shown an amazing aptitude for art: a handmade silk scarf for Amanda and the sweater, book and chocolate for Wade, who insisted on wearing his sweater.

Then she looked at her father.

"I have a gift for you, too, Dad." She retrieved a box from her room and handed it to him. "I always hoped I'd have the chance to give it to you."

Max opened the box and the album inside it, full of pictures of herself that Connie had assembled in chronological order. Tears seeped out of the corners of his tired eyes and ran down his haggard cheeks.

"It's the very best gift," he assured her. "But I have nothing for you."

"You've already given my Christmas gift to me,

Dad," Connie told him, hugging him close. "You're here."

"This is for my Daddy." Silver held a small, oddly wrapped package out to Wade.

Connie had helped her wrap a pair of socks they'd chosen together, but this wasn't it. She shrugged at Wade's questioning look.

"Merry Christmas, Daddy."

"Thank you, sweetheart." Wade took the package from her small hands and began unfolding the masses of tissue until he came to a piece of paper. He sucked in his breath. Then the proud man who'd guarded his heart for so long blinked away tears.

"Don't you like it?" Silver asked with a frown.

"I love it," he said setting the picture aside so he could wrap her in his arms. "I love you."

Connie leaned over to study Silver's drawing.

A little girl stood in what seemed to be a desert. There was a big black bird in the sky overhead, perhaps a vulture. An animal—maybe a coyote? hid behind a cactus, waiting. The sun was sinking behind the craggy mountains in the distance. But the little girl didn't seem afraid. She was smiling. Because coming toward her was a big strong man, and he held out one hand, asking her to take it.

"It's me and Daddy," Silver explained from her current perch on Wade's lap.

"It certainly is." Connie smiled, her heart full.

The rest of Christmas day passed in a blur of joy. David and Darla arrived with more gifts. Amanda announced she was giving Silver a pony, and Jared and Hornby showed up in time for dinner, which Amanda had taken over so Cora could be with her own family.

Much, much later when the guests had gone, after Silver had been tucked in and Max settled in a room on the main floor, Wade led Connie into the courtyard, by the pool. They stood in each other's arms and stared at the glittering stars twinkling against the inky blackness of the night.

"'For God so loved the world,'" Wade recited, "'that He gave his only son.' That was quite a gift."

"The very best gift," Connie agreed. "It's been a wonderful day. I can't thank you enough for finding my dad and getting him to come here. Or for my lovely ring." She held out her hand so the lantern reflected the dazzling sparkle of the diamond. "I love you," she whispered. "And I trust you—with my life."

"Me, too."

They stayed there until the soft, peach-colored light of dawn painted the eastern horizon and a melodic chorus of mourning doves, curve-billed thrashers and Gambel's quail melted into the air while raucous cactus wrens rat-a-tat-tats chimed in from a spiny cholla nearby.

"We should get some rest," Wade finally murmured.

"Yes." Connie frowned. "I forgot to ask you something."

"Oh?" He pushed the curls off her face and pressed a kiss against her forehead. "Ask away, my darling."

"What was in that letter?" Connie braced herself and whispered a prayer for courage.

"Let's find out." Wade pulled the envelope from his pocket. He hesitated before tearing it open. "Trust," he said out loud.

"Trust," Connie agreed.

Then he read the contents, his expression unreadable.

He was silent a long time.

"Wade?" Connie gripped his fingers. "Whatever it says doesn't matter. We'll deal with it together."

He folded the letter, shoved it back in his pocket and then turned to face her, his fingers spread through her hair, smoothing the strands. At last he spoke.

"The letter is a report about the man Bella ran away with. He couldn't be Silver's father. He wasn't able to have children." Wade stared into her eyes, his own shining with happiness.

"Thank God," Connie whispered.

"Thank God, indeed. God had it all worked out

before I even started worrying about it," he marveled. "Isn't that amazing?"

"And just like our Heavenly Father," Connie agreed. She hugged him fiercely. "So you are Silver's father."

"Well, the DNA tests aren't back," Wade reminded her. "But it really doesn't matter what they say because, yes, I am Silver's father." He grinned proudly, the shadows completely gone from his eyes. "Do you think she could be our flower girl?"

"You want to talk about our wedding already?" she asked in surprise.

"Our wedding can't come soon enough," Wade assured her. "Haven't you heard? My daughter and I are in love with our nanny."

* * * * *

Hello again!

I adore Christmas. Somehow the joy and hope of celebrating the Messiah's coming birth glows brighter every year. The happy carols, the wondrous gifts and the love of family and friends never grows old. I guess I'm a lot like Connie.

I hope you've enjoyed this first story in my new series, Love For All Seasons. Isn't it curious how we often allow fear and worry to steal the joy and peace we could have? Connie wants to find her dad, but her hopes stumble at the hurdles she comes to, as do Wade's when he faces up to his biggest fears. How great to know that this God of ours is big enough to handle any problems we encounter. Look for book 2 in this new series, coming in April.

During this blessed Christmas season, I'd love to hear from you. Contact me on my website: www.loisricher.com, or at Box 639, Nipawin, SK, Canada S0E 1E0. In the meantime, I wish you inner joy to carry you above the stressful moments. I wish you peace that can't be shattered. And I wish you love—the ageless, endless love of God that fills your heart just as fast as you give it away.

Merry Christmas to all!

Blessings,

Lois
Richer

QUESTIONS FOR DISCUSSION

1. Connie felt God led her to Tucson to find her father. Comment on ways we can discern God's leading in our own lives.

2. Consider Wade's situation. How should we as Christians react to such deep betrayal?

3. Amanda blamed Wade for her family's deaths. Suggest ways we may fault others as a means to lessening our own sense of loss or betrayal. What are some alternative ways to deal with our feelings of grief and loss?

4. Connie felt Wade needed to act as if Silver was his daughter until he learned differently. Do you agree? What suggestions would you have for someone in Wade's situation? Is blood truly thicker than water?

5. Connie used the internet as a resource for locating information about her father. Many adopted people do the same to find their birth parents. Discuss pros and cons of this approach and how it may impact the parent, who may be unprepared for a reunion with the child they left behind.

6. Eleven-year-old Connie felt abandoned by her father, Max, yet he had prepared a place for her to be cared for. Do you condone his actions? Suggest ways Christians can help people like Max who might need support but will not ask for it.

7. Silver desperately craved her father's love. List ways we can ensure our own children know they are loved and cherished, besides our actually telling them.

8. Connie desperately wanted the Abbots to find joy together at Christmas. Do you feel we sometimes place too much emphasis on having the perfect Christmas? List ways we can de-stress the holidays for family, friends and those we don't know.

9. Wade found a dinner at the center for the family to help with. At this dinner, Amanda discovered a measure of joy she hadn't realized she could share. Suggest some things we can do to assist those who find the Christmas season difficult and even painful.

10. Wade's friends were a great help in finding Connie's father. Discuss the importance of

friends and the roles you expect your friends to play in your own life.

11. Max did not want a reunion with Connie. He felt diminished—as if he'd failed her because he'd lost so much to cancer. Comment on ways we skew the truths in our own lives when reality becomes painful.

12. Connie withheld Wade's letter in hopes of saving the Abbots' Christmas. Wade didn't tell Connie about her father, because he wanted to surprise her. Discuss how good intentions can go awry and cause pain to those we love.

13. Wade's issue of trust took a long time to resolve. Consider how our actions can cause deep hurts in others.

14. Connie worked hard to create a wonderful Christmas for everyone. In the end she, too, experienced a joyful Christmas. Think about ways we can make Christmas more meaningful for ourselves and others by adjusting our attitudes.

15. Connie's mother passed on the Christmas spirit to her daughter through her actions.

Take a few moments to dwell on your Christmas habits and traditions. Consider the future. Will your children have a legacy they will carry on, one you've established? Is it too late to start one?

LARGER-PRINT BOOKS!

GET 2 FREE
LARGER-PRINT NOVELS
PLUS 2 FREE
MYSTERY GIFTS

Love Inspired®

Larger-print novels are now available...

LILP10R